Orgon Conclusion

by

I0535139

William Blackwell

Orgon Conclusion

Cover designed by Telemachus Press LLC
Published by Telemachus Press LLC
Paperback ISBN: 978-1-997835-00-4
Version: 2017.02.01

Acknowledgements

Heartfelt thanks to my loyal and supportive readers, friends and family, the hardworking staff at Telemachus Press, and Winslow Eliot. Special thanks to The Government of Prince Edward Island for its financial support.

To Donna Williams, for her unwavering loyalty, support and friendship

All our knowledge brings us nearer to our ignorance,
All our ignorance brings us nearer to death,
But nearness to death no nearer to God.
T.S. Eliot—*The Rock*
1934

Orgon Conclusion

Chapter One

"Damn, I wish I had done more with my life," Nathan Leer said to no one in particular. He sat alone on the main-floor balcony of his one-bedroom condo reflecting on his life. It was April Fool's Day.

And he felt like a fool.

He was unhappy with the direction of his life.

But actually he hadn't done all that badly considering his circumstances. Born to a poor, dysfunctional family in a tough lower-class neighborhood of Brantford, Ontario, he vividly remembered his father beating on his mother repeatedly.

He was six years old.

He felt defenseless. He wasn't, though. He remembered, during one such beating, he attacked his father, leaping on his back and pummeling him in the back of the head.

But all it took was a swift jerking motion, a left hook, and his father sent him flying across the room, crashing into the wall and crumpling to the floor.

Little wonder he left home when he was fifteen.

After experimenting with a myriad of drugs and violent involvement with street gangs, he quit school, packed his bags and headed to Vancouver, British Columbia, on the west coast of Canada. He wanted to see firsthand all the pristine beauty of nature he had read about.

Although he tried numerous jobs, he was too much of an independent thinker and could not fit into a nine-to-five routine. And, since he thought most of his bosses were not that bright, he had a problem with authority.

And his years growing up on the tough streets of Brantford had taught him never to take shit from anyone.

He had an edge.

A bit of a recluse, he didn't feel the need to seed his individual identity in with any group identity to accomplish a sense of self. Nathan had a sense of self, however fucked up it might be.

His thinking then, and now for that matter, was that if people didn't like the way he was then fuck them. Shit attitude, he knew, but it had served him well in the world.

He was a survivor.

If he had to psychoanalyze himself, and he often did, he would say the rejection he was dealt by his father (who always told him he wouldn't amount to shit) was being handed out to the rest of the world.

So for Nathan meeting people wasn't always that easy. If he felt someone invading his space, his reaction was not always positive. If he felt someone staring at him, unless perhaps it was a beautiful woman, his immediate reaction was not always to smile at them. He would frown, sometimes even glare, depending on his mood.

In spite of his tumultuous upbringing, he was happy with his own company, his own thoughts.

But he had tried to change, to be more positive, more people oriented.

After graduating from Simon Fraser University with a Bachelor of Arts degree, literature emphasis, Nathan started his own magazine distribution company.

A job that meant he had to talk to people. Which, he didn't much like but he managed well enough.

But it was a lonely existence. Driving his van, stopping at various venues. Mindless chitchat. Sign here. I'm getting the fuck outta' here. Sometimes he couldn't wait to finish the day so he could be by himself.

Oftentimes he'd sit in front of the television for hours. Other times he'd call a friend for a game of tennis or a beer. Although a loner, Nathan did have a few close friends. They loved him for his loyalty, off-the-wall sense of humor, and irreverent attitude about life.

Nathan didn't want too many friends. He had trust issues. Friends betrayed your trust.

He stirred from his contemplation. *Or am I wallowing in self-pity?* He reached for his pack of Colts Mild, slid one out and lit it, inhaling deeply.

Tastes like shit. He gazed out at the moon in the distance. The stars. Exhaled. *How nice it would be to escape the world of materialism.* A grey blanket of clouds rolled over the half-moon, obscuring the light. A lone white ray shone through a tiny pinhole in the bubble of clouds. Then, like a candle snuffed out, it was gone. The clouds passed and the moon brightened the night sky.

Make a plan. Organize yourself and get yourself out of this shit.

Along with his magazine distribution business, he was also a partner in Sal's, a failing coffee shop in the city center. He had foolishly borrowed against his properties, a riverfront acreage in BC and his apartment condo, and maxed his credit cards to buy a fifty percent ownership in the fledgling coffee shop.

He did this to bail a friend, Frank Hancock, out of a financial crisis. Combined with Nathan's poor management and the ailing BC economy, Sal's was taking a nose-dive. Nathan couldn't afford to take a dime out of it now, although the first year of operations it had performed admirably. And, in addition to subsidizing business debts with his other business income, he was also foolishly using credit card advances to pay the coffee shop debt.

As well, his interest in his relationship with his girlfriend Lena was beginning to wane. He loved her but thought they were very far apart intellectually.

Chapter Two

The phone rang, jarring him out of his thoughts. "Fuck off," he proclaimed loudly. It rang again. *Should I screen the call? Fuck it, I'll take it.* He walked into his apartment and picked up the ringing receiver.

"Hello," he said, trying his best to muster a positive voice.

"Nathan," Frank said. "Are you sitting down?"

He slumped into the couch. "I am now. What's up?"

"Sal's was broken into tonight. Someone crashed through our display window, made off with about $5,000 worth of cigarette inventory and about $4,000 worth of other shit."

"Fuck," said Nathan. "Are you there now?"

"Yeah. I've managed to get the window sealed off for now with plywood. The cops are coming in tomorrow to take a report. You should come in early tomorrow to do a cleanup. Call in an extra staff member if you have to."

Due to a rash of store break-ins in Vancouver, insurance companies had decided to discontinue covering tobacco inventory. The tobacco black market was booming. Increasingly, heroin junkies in need of a fix had turned to stealing and selling black market tobacco.

The city was getting worse.

Nathan looked at his watch: 2:56 am. He realized he had been sitting on his balcony feeling sorry for himself since about four that afternoon.

"I'll be in at six," he said. "I'll call Sarah to help me cleanup. Do we have insurance on the rest of the stuff and the window?"

"I think so. Listen, I'll be around tomorrow afternoon. We need to talk."

"Okay, see you tomorrow." *That's the third time the shop had been broken into*. Nathan walked to the fridge. Cracked a can of Kokanee beer. Took a long pull. Went to bed.

Chapter Three

Generally an insomniac, he drifted off in a matter of minutes. His dream was peaceful. He flew high above the Earth in a little white spaceship. He could see himself toiling at the sinking coffee shop, trying in vain to make it stay afloat and thrive. He saw a microcosm of his life, his relationships, friends, family. Everything flashed before him.

But he felt very far removed from it. He realized he was holding hands with a very strange-looking creature. Round face, white skin, big, beautiful green eyes. The eyes looked at him. Filled him with a sense of peacefulness, satisfaction.

The hand felt warm. The touch filled him with a euphoric sensation, like the prologue to a long and enjoyable orgasm.

He started to realize how trivial and insignificant his life was. How self-centered he was in his pursuit of material gain. How this all-encompassing love seemed so important. The face of the alien was not beautiful or ugly. Average. Big head. Smooth, thin, expressionless lips. But so full of love.

Ineffable.

But then the lips did form an expression. And it was one of overwhelming sadness and loss.

"Meeooow, meeooow, meeoow." Matty, Nathan's playful grey and white striped cat, was perched on top of his head, demanding her morning meal. He awoke with a grunt, gently sliding Meowing Matty off his head. He gave her an affectionate scratch and fed her. He loved that cat. Drearily, he staggered from the bed, the image of the alien still fresh in his mind.

Showered, dressed in jeans and a black golf shirt, he climbed into his black van and became one with the gridlock of traffic that flowed into downtown Vancouver.

He could not get those large omniscient eyes out of his mind.

Sal's was a disaster. *Be cool. Relax. Deep breaths.*

The thieves had smashed a large double-paned window, entered, and on their way to the cash register and cigarette inventory had collided with a display of expensive olive oils, balsamic vinegars, pickled onions, beets, antipasto. The floor was covered with broken glass and an oily red pond.

Sarah was busy serving customers, lining up for their morning coffee and muffin. Nathan nodded hello and got busy sweeping and mopping the oily mixture. He wanted to get it cleaned up quickly so no one would slip on it and sue his ass off.

His mind drifted back to the dream. *Those eyes. So much love. And so much sadness. What does it mean?* Nathan dreamt a lot, many of them containing violence and death. But, it seemed, he never remembered the dreams as clearly as this one. He still couldn't shake the feeling of euphoria that had accompanied her touch. It penetrated every inch of his body. And then the parting feeling. So sad. Seemed as if the creature wanted something from him, some sort of connection.

"Watch out," Nathan said, as a large fat man, two-liter Coke in hand, slipped on the oily mixture and careened helplessly into the rod iron display. On his way down he kicked the display and knocked an interesting mix of balsamic vinegar, olive oil and pickles on top of him. He sat in the mess, staring at Nathan helplessly. He still had his two-liter Coke intact in his hands. He had managed to save it.

Nathan rushed over to the man and tried to help him to his feet. He felt sorry for the guy.

"Are you okay?"

"Uhh, yeah." Examining himself. "Bit of a mess."

"Would you like a hand to the bathroom to get cleaned up?"

The man looked embarrassed. He wanted to leave. He braced himself on the rod iron pole that supported the display stand. With a jerking motion, hoisted himself up. There was a round of applause from customers who had gathered to see what all the fuss was about. The man, rather surprisingly, bowed as gracefully as he could. More whistles and cheers.

Sarah was laughing hysterically. Nathan was trying hard to contain an outburst of laughter. "I'm really very sorry we caused you all this trouble." But as he began to say more, the man set down his Coke and left the store. Nathan watched him leave, trailed by wet, sticky red footprints, relieved there wasn't any more of a scene.

Chapter Four

An hour later, Nathan had finished cleaning Sal's, filing a police report and an insurance claim. He sat with Frank in Rosie's café on Robson Street sipping a pint of Okanagan Pale Ale. The beer tasted good.

What Frank was saying even sounded good. A small, stalky man resembling a pit bull, Frank was discussing the possibility of selling Sal's. He owned two successful coffee shops and the one he owned with Nathan was the proverbial monkey on his back.

He wanted it to disappear.

Nathan was over-leveraged going in, although he had managed a successful sub-lease of the business just recently, which had bought them a little more time. But he wasn't spending enough time growing the business.

And it was beginning to show. The money out always seemed to be higher than the money in. As well, a few battles of late with Frank, who had a nasty temper and could be quite explosive, had curtailed his interest level.

Nathan was content to go to hell in a hand basket. At least he was enjoying the ride.

Or am I?

He smiled a bit at that notion as Frank continued. "We both know sales are not what they used to be. You're not spending enough time there. Much of the Asian contingent that made up a large part of our market has left the country. People are not spending as much. BC is heading into a recession. The writing is on the wall, buddy," looking Nathan square in the eyes. "We have to sell."

"Let's do it. Do you want me to take a crack at it or would you like to list with a realtor?"

Frank considered this. He knew this particular partnership hadn't worked out that well. But Nathan had injected some much needed cash into his business at a time when he was four months behind in lease payments. Nathan had bailed him out just as the bailiff was about to lock him out of one of his other successful coffee shops. Frank also knew Nathan to be very articulate and a shrewd negotiator.

"Go for it, Nathan. You can probably sell it. Advertise in the *Chinese Times* and the *Vancouver Sun*. Try it for a month. If you can't get anything serious, we'll list it."

Nathan jotted down a few notes and picked up his cell. He made two quick calls, placed two classified ads. "Done."

Frank smiled. One thing he liked about Nathan. When he put his mind to something, he did it.

They ordered another drink and discussed other things. "How's Lena?" Frank asked.

"Uhh, haven't talked to her in a couple of days. Should call her." Nathan had been so caught up in his business woes he hadn't given his relationship much thought. He picked up the cell phone. Frank seemed only moderately interested in the conversation. What had caught his attention was an attractive brunette standing at the bar, between sips of her drink, glancing at him. She had deep green eyes, an olive-toned complexion and a sexy smile. And, she had nice curves.

"Hello, honey," Nathan said after Lena answered. "How are you?"

"Groovy, baby, just groovy." It was the way Lena talked.

"Sorry I haven't called lately. Been a little preoccupied. What are you up to?"

"Watching Beverly Hills 90210, and then Melrose Place."

Nathan hated those two shows. One dimensional characters. All gorgeous. Little, if any depth to the characters or dialogue. However, he had watched them many nights just to please Lena.

"And you? Where are you?"

"I'm with Frank at Rosie's. Just finished a beer and a meeting. Can I see you tonight?"

"Sorry, honey. My mom is coming by later and we're going shopping. You can take me out to Milestones restaurant on the weekend if you like." It seemed to Nathan all they did was go to Milestones on the weekend. Lena was a sweet woman. Just intellectually, she couldn't keep up with Nathan. And she was a little immature. But she had a quirky sense of humor and could make him laugh. Standing just over five feet tall, she had short blonde hair, blue eyes, a smattering of freckles and cute little dimples. Although she was thirty-two, she could easily pass for twenty-two. He had been with her for a little over two years.

"Sure, sweetie, I'll call you," Nathan said.

"I love you," Lena said.

"Love you too. Bye." Nathan clicked the cell phone off and put it down. Then he began to think of Lena's ample breasts and he felt a stirring in his loins.

Frank, meanwhile, was at the bar chatting up the brunette. He had already bought her a drink. Bit of a ladies' man, he was. Nathan eyed the woman's legs. *Shapely. Wonder what her breasts are like?*

Nathan stood up, waved at Frank and left.

Chapter Five

Outside it was getting dark. Thunder boomed and it started raining. He ran the three blocks to Sal's. Was drenched by the time he arrived. When he entered he saw Sarah (some customers preferred to call her Scara) and her punk rock friend, both leaning on the counter, blocking passage for customers.

Nathan didn't say anything. That was one of his other problems. Sometimes he was too easy going.

They both had their noses pierced. Scara's friend cast Nathan a dirty look.

He ignored it. "How are things going?"

"Been slow. All the customers seem really weird tonight. I'm tired. Since I got here so early, can I go home early?"

"Go ahead," Nathan said. "I'll finish the shift and lock up. Thanks for coming in." As Scara left, Nathan wondered about his ability to pick good staff.

Business was slow. Time dragged. The rain had cleared the streets and the few customers that did come in were old faithful. They were getting fewer by the day.

Just as Nathan began to think it would be an uneventful night, Jisumi walked in. The one person he did not want to see. Nathan had dated her and slept with her once a few years back.

Now, the diminutive Asian woman had taken up the part-time hobby of stalking him. It was unnerving, particularly tonight. Jisumi would make a guest appearance at the coffee shop at least once a month. She also frequently phoned Nathan and occasionally would turn up at his apartment. She smiled, approaching the cash register with her coffee.

She had very bad body odor.

Nathan cringed, but tried to appear calm. "Hi Jisumi. Nice to see you." He fidgeted with some elastic bands as he rang in her coffee. She didn't say anything. She took her change, carried her coffee to a bar stool by the window and sat down.

She cast him a pained glance. "I miss you so much, why you no call me?"

"Jisumi, we've been through all this. We're just friends remember. It's been over a year. You know I have a girlfriend."

Jisumi winced. She slowly regained her composure and continued to stare at Nathan.

Nathan fidgeted with the elastic bands. The night dragged. Jisumi stared.

Finally, five minutes to ten, closing time. *Time to get rid of her.*

"Listen Jisumi, I'm closing the shop. I'm sorry but you'll have to leave now."

"I wait. We go together."

Unable to think of a response, he went about his closing duties, washing coffee containers, cashing out.

She began walking the aisles. She stopped behind a potato chip display. Nathan saw her staring at him from behind the display. He was really freaked out now. He felt scared. He approached her.

"Look you've got to get out of here. Please I'm closing, can you go?" Jisumi burst into tears. She ran into the washroom. Nathan thought about calling security to haul her out of the store. He didn't.

He finished cashing out, cleaning. He walked to the bathroom to see if he could coax her out. He knocked on the door. Whimpering sounds could be heard.

"Jisumi, are you okay?" Nothing. He waited a few minutes. He tried the door. It was open. He opened it, peered in. She lay on the floor behind the toilet in a fetal position. Tears streamed down her face. She sobbed. Nathan felt bad.

He walked to the front counter. Called building security. Rent-a-cops were not supposed to physically handle problem patrons. They could be charged with assault. But Chris was different. Nathan had befriended him, offering him free coffee and donuts. Chris was a wannabe cop. A tough guy. He told Nathan if he ever needed anyone physically removed to call him. He had Chris on the line. "Chris, I've got a situation here. I have a woman curled up in the fetal position behind the toilet in the woman's washroom. Could you please remove her?"

"Is it Jisumi?" Chris had been briefed on the stalker.

"Yeah."

"Be right there," Chris said without hesitation.

Moments later, Jisumi, kicking, screaming, and crying, was carried out of the store by two security guards. They set her down on the sidewalk and after a few minutes, she stood up and walked away. Nathan gave them free soft drinks and donuts, thanked them profusely, finished cashing out, and before locking the shop peered outside for a few seconds to see if Jisumi had returned.

The coast was clear so he locked the door and left, walking hastily to his van parked in a nearby commercial zone. He kept looking over his shoulder to see if Jisumi was following him. She was nowhere in sight. He unlocked the passenger door first, loaded in some miscellaneous grocery items. He was low on cash so he had resorted to taking food instead of wages from the shop when he needed groceries.

He climbed in and started the engine. As he pulled away, Jisumi appeared. He gunned it. There was too much traffic. She gained on the van, reaching for the passenger door, trying to open it.

Shit. I forgot to lock it. Just as Jisumi pulled on the door handle, Nathan reached over with his fist, slamming the door lock down.

Just in time.

He was now on Robson Street and Jisumi ran beside the van, gripping the door handle. "We go together," she said. They were attracting a lot of attention. Nathan waited for a break in traffic. He got it and accelerated. Jisumi let go of the door handle. He weaved through some cars. He could see her in the rearview mirror, running down the middle of Robson Street, flailing her arms, yelling, oblivious to the traffic. He turned a corner and she was out of sight.

His hands shook at the wheel.

In his apartment, he closed all the blinds, disconnected the phone, turned off all the lights, sat on his couch, drinking a beer. *Definitely not the best day I've had.* His hands still trembled.

Chapter Six

Sleep came easily again for Nathan. He was exhausted, physically and mentally. The dream returned. He found himself being swept away to his acreage retreat, about four hours north of Vancouver. When his businesses were going well, he used to camp at this magical spot almost every weekend. Situated in the mountains, about three thousand feet above sea level, the rectangular-shaped property had a river running through it. There was a 19-foot camper trailer, an outhouse, and a foundation, more like a large deck, for a cabin he and his friends had constructed in better days.

Just being there calmed him immensely. He had an affinity with nature. Birds would occasionally fly out of nowhere and land in his hand, at his calling. His friends were amazed at this. The birds would look at him for a few seconds, minutes sometimes, and then fly away.

He had had many encounters with bears, his favorite animal. He had no fear of them. When he encountered them, they would stare at each other and usually the bears would lumber away. Or, Nathan would walk away. He was fascinated by their size, and he always thought they were far more intelligent than they were given credit for.

Now he sat beside his favorite fire pit, a blaze raging, flames licking at the sky. He studied the flames. They seemed to hold some meaning, indecipherable to him. *Was it the eyes? Were the eyes in the fire?* He strained to see the eyes.

He could almost feel them looking at him. Then he could see them. They grew bigger and filled him with a sense of calm and inner peace, something he thought so many people strive for but few manage to attain. *Too much selfish preoccupation with material gain.*

He was mesmerized by the eyes. Green eyes. Suddenly he was swept away in the same spaceship, along with the eyes, high above the acreage.

He felt a warm hand holding his. He looked. The same being he had dreamt of the night before. He searched the eyes. The being had a feminine quality. She smiled at him, a warm comforting smile. He watched the fire become a small red circle and eventually disappear from sight. The Earth became smaller as he soared higher into space.

"I have something to show you," the eyes told him. He wondered how he could understand the eyes, as the lips didn't move.

Now, he was floating down, toward a lush green planet, dotted with white mushroom-shaped buildings. Little white creatures in air gliders flew around on a series of weaving and interlocking air highways. The machines resembled snowmobiles, but much sleeker and with glass-enclosed cockpits. A complex of large, multi-storied buildings stood out. *Administration buildings. Government.*

He didn't remember landing, but he was led into an ornate building. Massive interior. He couldn't see the ceilings. A white staircase was in the middle of the room, spiraling up into a white mist. The mist was faintly lit by a deep green color that seemed to flash in synchronicity with his heartbeat. He could feel his heartbeat, hear it thumping.

Now, he stood at the top of this plateau, the mist enveloping him. He noticed the eyes were no longer with him. The hand no longer held his.

The mist felt comfortable. His heartbeat slowed. The green color came in rhythmic waves. The mist cleared. A tower stood in front of him. On top of it, perched on an ornate throne, was a small bald man. He was a stark white color but for his deep green, large and penetrating eyes.

The rest of the man's facial features were obscured by the mist. If he even had any other features, Nathan couldn't be sure.

All he could see were the glowing eyes. It warmed Nathan. The eyes spoke to him. "We have studied humankind for over one hundred years. Now, we need a human being to live on our planet, to observe, and to learn the ways that love can change. This person will eventually return to Earth to spread these teachings to the rest of the world, making your world a better place to live. You are the person we have chosen."

Now Nathan was getting a little rattled. *I'm no fuckin' proselytizer. Let someone else have the job. Besides, I'm dreaming. I'll wake up with the same stress and problems I had before.*

"This is no dream," the eyes said, reading his mind. He felt a stinging sensation on the palm of his hand and he examined it. A small white circle appeared, no bigger than the head of a thumb tack. He wiped his hand nervously, trying to erase the circle. It remained, but the stinging sensation faded.

The eyes continued. "We have watched patiently the human species. You destroy your planet and kill each other. Most times you are motivated by greed, selfishness, the pursuit of material possessions. You steal, lie and cheat. Your kind has lost sight of what really matters: Love, respect, kindness, caring for your fellow man, nature and respecting the animals of your planet."

"Maybe we have," Nathan retorted. He was tired of this dream and wanted to wake up. He didn't want any agenda that had to do with saving the planet. "Not my problem, though."

Chapter Seven

He woke precipitously. Matty was on his forehead, licking his nose. He scratched her affectionately, placed her gently on the side of the bed. He smelled burnt wood. His right palm was itchy. He looked at it and saw a small white circle. At that, he bolted upright in bed.

He cleared his head, told himself it was only a dream. He would look at his palm again and the white circle would be gone. He looked. It was still there. The smell of burnt embers remained.

The phone rang. A guy named John. From the classified ad. He wanted a meeting to discuss purchasing Sal's. Nathan set the meeting for five that afternoon at Rosie's and hung up. *Better be quick. My rent at Sal's is due in a week and I'm broke.*

His credit cards were maxed and the magazine distribution business wasn't bringing in enough to cover his living expenses. He also had a mortgage payment due in a week.

It would take a while for foreclosure proceedings, but he knew it was inevitable. He was about to hit the wall financially.

Emotionally he didn't feel that great either.

The phone rang again. He picked it up. "Hello," he said into the receiver, trying to disguise an impending feeling of doom.

"Nathan, buddy, how are you?" It was Michelle Barcley, a longtime friend.

"Hey, Michelle. Good. And you?"

They exchanged some perfunctory chit-chat about what they'd been up to lately and then Michelle got to the point.

"There's drop-in volleyball at the gym on Robson Street tonight if you're interested. I booked a spot for us. It's at eight. Lena will be there. I just got off the phone with her."

Nathan thought a little physical activity might be a good way to work off some stress. *Better that than booze.* "Sure, I'll be there. Guess I should call Lena and see if she needs a ride."

There was a short pause.

"Uh, I don't think you have to worry about that."

Michelle explained, as tactfully as possible—two guys, twins, had moved into a house next to Lena's rented apartment on the north shore. Lately, she had been seeing a lot of them and one in particular she had taken a shine to. They would be driving her to volleyball.

Disappointed, Nathan struggled to comprehend this. His head started pounding. In spite of their intellectual differences, he loved her.

Or so he thought.

Michelle tried to reassure him it was just a phase she was going through and she would get over it. He didn't feel that reassured but he agreed to show up and see what, if anything, was going on.

Chapter Eight

Nathan's mind was not on work as he weaved through the downtown traffic in his 1992 Chevy van. The white circle on his hand, his girlfriend's new found love interests, his dire financial situation. The upcoming meeting about Sal's.

He made six deliveries, parked in a commercially-zoned alley across the street from Sal's. He couldn't shake the image of the white bald man in his dream and he could still smell burning embers. And the circle mystified him. *That wasn't a dream. That was real. What the hell is going on here?*

About an hour later, he was sitting on Rosie's patio with Frank, John and Paul.

In their matching black suits, the two resembled a couple of Xerox copies, or clones.

They had toured the store (it was advertised for $150,000) and briefly reviewed the financials, lease, and inventory.

Over cigarette smoke and drinks, John said: "It actually looks like a location with potential."

Am I hearing right? The first people to view the business and they're talking about potential.

John continued. "Of course if we decided to do anything, we would put together a contract subject to verification of all the sales records and financials for the past year, as well as a condition that an associate of ours sit in the store for a week to verify the sales numbers."

"That's fine," said Frank. "We haven't even talked about price."

"We won't talk price at all this evening," Paul said. "We're going to talk about it tonight, to see if we're even interested. We'll be in touch tomorrow or the next day."

Everyone stood and shook hands. When Nathan shook hands with John and Paul, he noticed their expressions changed instantly from serious to delighted. He didn't understand. While Frank sat across from him sipping his Okanagan Pale Ale and puffing on his Marborough, Nathan examined his hand. The white circle was still there but its glow had dimmed slightly.

"What're you looking at, Nathan?" Frank snapped him out of his thoughts "Those guys have dirty hands or something?"

"Uh, nothing," Nathan said. "Just thinking about something."

"Well start thinking about selling our business. We don't have the money to pay rent. Did you see how those guy's faces lit up after they shook hands with you? I think they're going to make an offer. We should adjust cash register tapes first thing every morning to show a few hundred more in sales so we can put this deal together."

Nathan didn't like the sound of that. But he also knew that almost everyone who sold retail businesses doctored the books. The daily sales always looked better than they actually were. And what choice did he have? They were in dire straits. He nodded. They paid the bill and walked across the street to Sal's.

Gloria, Frank's Mexican girlfriend, was working at the shop, filling in for an employee who had called in sick. Nathan checked the time. He had forty-five minutes before he had to face Lena, the twins, and volleyball.

Gloria was in tears when they entered. Frank ran to her aid. She pointed outside at a man who had just left. "That guy there was rude to me for no reason and he called me a fucking slut."

Frank was capable of exploding for a hell of a lot less. Nathan had been on the receiving end of his abusive temper more than a few times. Frank flew out the door and confronted the man, a rather disheveled sort, but tall and muscular.

After some animated discussion, Frank started punching him in the face. His coffee splattered on the ground. People were beginning to gather. The man fell to the ground and Frank mounted him, pummeling him repeatedly in the face. Blood squirted from his nose and mouth.

The guy didn't stand a chance against the raging pit bull.

Nathan had seen enough.

He bent down, grabbed Frank's arm. "Fuck off," Frank yelled. The man was on the concrete, bleeding. Onlookers gawked. Then Frank's demeanor changed. He smiled, calmed down instantly and stared at his victim sympathetically.

"Listen, I'm real sorry about that," Frank said, helping the strung-out heroin addict to his feet.

He brought him into the shop washroom, bandaged his cuts, gave him a coffee and a muffin and bid him farewell. The man, dumbfounded by this act of kindness, uttered an apology and left.

The crowd of onlookers whistled and applauded. Frank looked a little out of sorts. He was trying to understand why he had been so nice. But he still had a smile on his face, more like a shit-eating grin really. Nathan had watched him beat up people before without even an inkling of remorse or conscience.

This was strange behavior for Frank. Then Nathan remembered the white circle and its effect on the suits. He looked at his hand. It was now only a faint glow.

Chapter Nine

With his gym bag in tow, Nathan entered the Robson Street gym. Located on the second floor with glass-paned walls framing the exterior, it had a bar, relaxing lounge chairs, tables, a few dart boards, pool tables, air hockey, and four glass-enclosed volleyball courts.

It was managed by a jovial Chinese man, who was always joking around. Last year, Nathan had played there every Thursday with a group of his friends.

Michelle was the organizer. She organized all social functions and brought people together. It was what she liked to do.

As he walked in, he noticed Michelle and her boyfriend Stephen first and said hello. He saw Lena sitting in a lounge chair being doted on by the twins. She was enthralled by their attention. Young, good-looking blonde guys in their mid-twenties. One enjoyed his view of Lena's ample breasts, staring at her cleavage and smiling as they talked.

Lena rose from her chair when she noticed him. "Oh, don't get up on my account," Nathan said sarcastically. He had the capacity to be an asshole.

She approached, ignoring the comment and pecked him on the cheek. She introduced the two studs as Dalton and Walton. But Nathan wasn't listening. His mind was swimming with emotion.

He bit his tongue, changed, and hit the court. He would have an opportunity to talk to her later.

They played volleyball and Lena openly flirted with the twins, allowing them to grab her in places that were typically reserved for a significant other. Naturally athletic, Nathan had a wicked spike and serve. Two opportunities presented themselves and he took advantage of both, one to hammer a spike off the nose of Walton and another slammed into Dalton's eye.

Surprisingly, they took it good-naturedly and Nathan felt bad about it later. *It wasn't their fault after all, was it? It was Lena's fault.*

He needed to talk to her.

The opportunity presented itself. After three games, they took a break. Nathan saw Lena approach the bar and followed. He gently grabbed her arm. "Listen, we need to talk."

"Oh. About what?"

Nathan tried to contain himself. "Do you think that's cool what you're doing out there on the court, openly flirting with those guys? If you don't want to be with me why don't you just tell me?"

"They're just friends. Calm down. They're my new neighbors and I'm just showing them some Vancouver hospitality."

"Michelle tells me you have a crush on one of them and he's been over to your house a few times," Nathan said, balling his fists and narrowing his eyes.

"Look, I don't want to talk about this because there is nothing to talk about," Lena insisted.

"Fine. If there's nothing to talk about now then there's nothing to talk about—ever! It's over. I'm not going to put up with this shit."

"Wait," she pleaded.

But before she could say more, Nathan, still in his shorts and t-shirt, grabbed his gym bag and left.

Chapter Ten

Driving home, all he could think about was what a bitch she had been. Nathan was crushed. Totally devastated. His head hurt. He felt like he was losing his mind at that moment, just barely clinging onto the edge of sanity.

So much had gone wrong lately and it was taking a toll.

He stopped and bought a case of beer and two packs of Colts Mild. *I'll go home and drink and smoke my brains out. Who says you can't drown your sorrows in alcohol? Whoever it was, they're sadly mistaken.*

That night, he drank eighteen beers, smoked an entire pack of Colts Mild, and passed out on the couch, beer can empties strewn all over the carpet.

His dream was bleak. He was getting dragged down into a spiraling, fiery black hole. During the descent, hundreds of images of death, suffering, bloodshed, murder, flashed around him, all-encompassing. He heard gut-wrenching screams.

He reached the bottom of a fiery pit and landed with a thud on a dungeon-like floor. He stood up. Flames flickered everywhere. In one dark corner, he saw a man being flogged with a cat o' nine tails whip, screaming.

Another corner, orgiastic frenzy.

Another black room, deformed midgets raping a half-naked, screaming young woman.

Nathan thought his head was going to explode. *So much chaos, violence. I've died and gone to hell. Drank too much beer. Alcohol poisoning. Dead.*

In the midst of the chaos, he heard footsteps approaching. He was sure he was dreaming. But, he couldn't wake up.

A tall man with black hair, goatee and chiseled features stood before him. He wore a black suit and was well groomed. He had mysterious, yellowish red eyes that glowed.

"I'm glad you could come down and pay us a visit, Nathan. I'm Beal."

Nathan didn't know what to say. Beal grabbed his hand, escorted him into a dimly lit room, fiery torches illuminating each corner. They sat on black leather arm chairs.

He could barely see two naked women fondling each other lovingly on a king-sized bed adorned with burning candles.

"We have certain enemies that we believe you have been in contact with. These fools believe they can change the fundamental nature of mankind. They think they can change the evil course of self-destruction mankind has embarked on. Evil is an inherent part of human nature. Everyone has the capacity for it," Beal said.

One of the women rose from the bed, approached seductively, put her arms around Beal, rubbing her well-shaped breasts tantalizingly against his back. She had a mane of thick black hair, a curvaceous body, an evil grin and soft features.

She smiled at Nathan. He felt a stirring in his loins.

"We do not want you to accept what these aliens are offering you. We can offer you much more. Unlimited money, power, all the beautiful women you want."

"This is crazy. I'm dreaming."

"No," Beal said. "You're not. As a gesture of good faith, I offer you these two beautiful women. Have your way with them. Think about what I said. If you decline, your life will be in serious jeopardy."

It already is.

Beal left, leaving Nathan alone with the women. The shrill screams of the damned echoed through the halls.

One of the woman fondled Nathan through his pants. He tried to resist but the temptation was too strong and he had his way with them, experiencing intense sexual pleasure the likes of which he was sure he never had before.

Chapter Eleven

The phone rang. Nathan's head thudded. He opened his eyes. He had fallen off the couch in his sleep. He woke to the mess of beer cans, gently pushed Matty away and crawled to the phone, glancing at the time: 1:45 p.m.

"Hello."

"Nathan, how's it going?"

"Hi Dave." It was his long-time friend Dave Healy, who lived two blocks away from Nathan's apartment. It was Saturday. They usually played tennis on Saturday.

"Jeez you sound rough. Drinking last night?"

"A little."

"So, are you up for a game?" The courts were within walking distance.

"Uh, yeah sure. Listen I need to sleep a few more hours. How about I meet you there at four-thirty?"

"See you there," Dave said, and hung up.

Nathan slept until four, showered, threw on a ripped white t-shirt, an old pair of blue shorts and left.

The April air smelled fresh and the sun warmed him as he walked. His head still ached but the pain had subsided a little after he had popped two Advils.

Memories of Lena and the experience with Beal and his seductresses intermingled in his mind creating bittersweet emotions. *The dream. Was it a dream?* When he woke his briefs were halfway to his knees.

And, in spite of all the heartache and worry, he felt deeply sexually satisfied.

On the courts, sun shining, whacking the ball, practicing his forehand, his backhand, Nathan started feeling a little better. Dave, on the other end of the court, had a powerful forehand, was tall and lanky with very good reach. The two were fairly evenly matched. They didn't keep score, just rallied the ball for exercise. Their skill level was very high.

After tennis, they sat in Dave's apartment drinking beer, a decent one-bedroom unit on the second floor of a stucco building containing five other similar suites. Nathan wouldn't overdo it tonight. He would have three at the most and go home to bed, he decided.

There was a lot going on in his mind that he needed to sort out.

He told Dave about the situation at Sal's, his dire financial situation, the break-up with Lena and the strange dreams he had been having lately including the white circle and the highly sexual nightmare last night. Dave was one of his closest friends and he had to tell somebody.

"Sounds like a struggle between the forces of good and evil," Dave said skeptically.

"Look at this." Nathan exposed his palm. The circle was barely visible.

Dave examined it without touching it. "Weird." But he wasn't buying the story. "You sure it isn't something left over from some white powder you've been snorting? Or one of your circle jerks?"

Nathan had tried cocaine only a few times. Recreationally. Didn't like the drug, the depressing feeling coming down from it, and the strong craving for more. Highly damaging and addictive. "I haven't touched cocaine in years." He couldn't help himself from smiling at the second question, but decided not to justify it with a response.

"Look, these ... aliens want me to go to their planet, teach me how love can save the world, and come back down to Earth to proselytize about the healing power of love." Nathan realized how ridiculous it sounded.

"That sounds like some wacked out science fiction movie, Nathan. You should hear yourself talking. Listen, you're under a lot of stress right now. You've always had lots of weird and freaky nightmares. It's just another one. Put it out of your mind and concentrate on selling your business to save your soul."

"No, it's a little more than that," Nathan insisted. "I feel like I'm being pulled in two different directions here, like it's some kind of a test of my moral fiber. Like I could get pulled down into an abyss or I could rise above the whole mess and reach a state of inner peace."

"Everyone gets pulled in different directions in their lives. And they have to decide which way they want to go. But you're putting some kind of an epic twist on this whole thing which I'm not sure is really there."

"You're not sure? That means you don't think I'm crazy, right?" With all that had happened lately, Nathan had thought he might be losing his grip on reality. That he had concocted the whole thing.

"You've never been much of a bullshitter," Dave said. "So I guess, you're either losing it or these things could have happened. But who would believe that you've got some aliens who want you to live with them and on the other hand you've got some servant of Satan pulling you in another direction?

You better not tell any of this shit to anyone else, if you don't want to get committed to a nuthouse."

Nathan paused, sipping his beer. He felt sick.

Dave tried to talk him into going out to the Fairview on Broadway, one of his favorite bars for picking up cougars. Nathan didn't want any part of it and went home to sleep.

Chapter Twelve

Two weeks had passed. Nathan hadn't been able to close the suits on the sale of Sal's. About three other meetings with other potential buyers had ended dismally. Sal's was in arrears and the landlord was threatening to send in a bailiff to lock the doors.

Sales were about $250 per day but the coffee shop needed to pull in at least $600 daily to break even. Numerous creditors were calling. It had reached the point that Nathan wouldn't answer his business line when it rang. Or, if he did answer it, he would say, "The manager isn't in."

At one point, Dave came into the store and started fielding calls and even threatening the odd bill collector with physical violence. Dave had a dark side. He had the propensity for violence.

Nathan's personal financial situation wasn't much better. He had now maxed his credit cards to over fifty thousand dollars and could no longer afford to make the minimum payments. His mortgage arrears were mounting and the bank manager was no longer his best friend.

He was drinking much more than he wanted to admit.

His ex had called a few times and he had ignored most of the calls. He had picked up during a drunken binge and remembered saying something about remaining friends. He couldn't remember what else they might have discussed.

His mind flitted from one thought to the next as he drove to a meeting with Frank. He had completed seven magazine deliveries. He parked in an alley behind Granville Street.

He walked across the street to Sal's on Granville, one of Frank's successful locations. With monthly lease costs of about three thousand and daily sales upwards of two thousand dollars, it was easy to understand why the coffee shop was so profitable.

He wasn't looking forward to the meeting. Frank's tone of voice on the phone earlier had sounded less than inviting.

In the past two weeks, Nathan couldn't remember a single dream. He wondered now if his mind had made up the whole thing. He also noticed the circle had disappeared.

Nathan and Frank sat outside Sal's at a table with an umbrella, sipping coffee. A drizzly, gray day. Yet the streets were alive with the usual mix; business types, shoppers and couples strolling arm in arm. The street freaks were out as well: Beggars, junkies, loud and obnoxious punkers and drunks.

Granville Street was a hub of activity. Night clubs, pubs, convenience stores, coffee shops, and a few porn shops which, along with the riff-raff, leant a seedy edge to the street. But it was beginning to show signs of revitalization. Frank had wisely secured a retail storefront lease and built another Sal's.

They talked about the dismal financial situation of Sal's, Robson Street, the partnership. Frank felt it was time to list it with a commercial real estate broker.

Puffing on his smoke, he said, "I have a guy who can list it today. He charges a ten percent flat commission."

"Go ahead," Nathan said, looking out of the corner of his eye at a rather voluptuous blonde walking past the shop. "Just make sure you specify in the contract that seller's rights are reserved. I still have ads running. You never know, the suits may return."

Frank agreed to look after it, disappearing inside his coffee shop. Nathan stayed outside, sipping on his coffee and smoking a cigar.

The meeting hadn't gone that badly.

Nathan noticed a woman perhaps twenty-eight sitting across from him. She had smart brown eyes, flowing brunette hair, and mulatto skin. She looked Latin American, probably Mexican. He had travelled through Mexico and knew how to speak a little Spanish. She smiled at Nathan as she sipped her coffee and he returned the smile. *She's hot.*

On an impulse, he walked over to her table, introduced himself and asked if he could join her.

"Sure," she said, waving him to a chair.

Nathan sat. Her name was Adelita. "Are you new to Vancouver?"

"Yes, just arrived about seven months ago. Been living on Vancouver Island with a friend of mine. I'm just here for the weekend."

Her English was pretty good. He was instantly attracted to her. They talked for about a half hour. Nathan learned that Adelita used to have an art business in Mexico City. She sold her father's paintings. She planned on relocating to Canada to ply her trade and was currently sorting it out with Canadian immigration officials.

He told her about his different businesses, that Frank was his business partner, deliberately omitting his financial crisis. The sound of Adelita's voice was music to his ears. *It's amazing how quickly men fall in love. Or was it lust?* He liked how easily she smiled, how she laughed at his jokes, and her zest for life. It was what he needed to pull himself out of his stressful situation.

The question was could he handle it?

Chapter Thirteen

A week later and spring was starting to give way to warmer temperatures of summer. Nathan had been out with Adelita three times. Two dinners, walks along the beach at Stanley Park. Things were going well with his new relationship and very poorly with his businesses.

He had slowed his drinking, but his financial situation was worsening.

His ex-girlfriend Lena had called a few more times, wanting to renew the relationship. Nathan would have no part of it but politely told her he would call soon and they would have coffee or a drink.

He had no intention of following up.

Adelita had not been around the times that Lena had called. *That was lucky. She seems like the jealous type.* He knew from previous relationships with Mexican women that they had fiery tempers and could be insanely jealous. *Must run in the genes.*

They weaved along the Sea-To-Sky highway toward Whistler. Their trip would take them through Pemberton valley, where they would take the Hurley River Road to the little mining town of Bralorne and nearby, the acreage—paradise on Earth.

Nathan gazed out at the tranquil blue ocean as he drove. It was a sunny day with a few puffy white clouds lazily drifting by. He smoked his cigar, took in the spectacular view.

Adelita enjoyed the drive too. Occasionally she would comment on some bit of scenery and how beautiful it was.

"Wait until we get to Bralorne, sweetie," Nathan said, smiling at her. "It's absolutely incredible there." She looked at him, smiled, put her hand in his. *The world is right,* Nathan thought, forgetting about his problems.

After a few minutes of blissful silence, Adelita said, "I'm a little concerned about you."

We've only been dating a short time and she's concerned about me? She must know about the failing business or something. "Oh ... what are you concerned about?"

"I went to your shop the other day to see you. While I was buying a coffee there was some man demanding money from the cashier. Said his company was owed three thousand dollars and it hadn't been paid for over three months. He looked legitimate."

"Oh, he's for real all right," Nathan said. He didn't see the point in lying. She wasn't stupid and had probably figured a lot of his mess out by now anyway.

"Are you in some kind of trouble?"

"We haven't had the customers we normally do. The business is doing poorly. We're trying to sell it, get rid of it before it goes under. We're a sinking ship." Nathan hadn't yet mentioned his mortgage arrears or credit card debt. Things were rapidly getting worse.

Adelita seemed gravely concerned. Her brow furrowed. "Is there something I can do to help?"

Nathan was touched by her concern. And, he had to admit, in such a short amount of time, he was madly in love with Adelita. Lena stilled played on his mind, and he wondered if Adelita was a transition girl. *No, this is the real thing.* He didn't want to borrow Adelita's money. He knew she didn't have much. But the bank was now pressing him on his condo arrears, threatening to foreclose if a payment wasn't made soon.

Yet he also knew she needed as much money as possible to get into Canada.

She had a lawyer working on her refugee status. According to her story, and Nathan didn't know how much of it to believe, she had taken up the cause of Mayan Indian farmers in the state of Chiapas, an armed rebellion that had erupted in 1994. They wanted greater autonomy from the government, the preservation of their culture and social reforms. They were viewed as rebels, and due to Adelita's involvement with them, someone in Mexico wanted her dead.

Nathan scratched his brow as he drove. He knew $1,000 would buy him a little time, at least as far as his condo was concerned. He had an idea. Adelita lived in Victoria, on Vancouver Island, but wanted to move to Vancouver. *What the hell. It's worth a shot.*

"Why don't you move in with me, maybe put $1,000 toward some rent? See how things go with us. You know I'm crazy in love with you."

She smiled and gazed into his eyes. She was in love. "This could be a little premature," she said.

"We'll you can stay for a few months until you find an apartment, if you like."

Adelita was still looking for a job, someone who would pay her illegally until she could get legitimate status in Canada. But she knew Vancouver had more opportunities than Victoria, and she was interested in seeing a lot of Nathan.

She agreed, leaned over and kissed him. He smiled and drove.

They stopped in Squamish and ate a couple of Big Macs. Continued on past Whistler, the world-famous ski resort. Then into Pemberton, where they drove through the valley until they came to Hurley River Road. This summer access gravel road winds its way up through the mountains switchback style. Some sections are quite narrow and dangerous, and the road, in many spots, veers dangerously close to the mountain's edge. But the scenery is breathtaking. Panoramic views, mountain rivers and creeks, lush forest, an abundance of wildlife. Raw wilderness. Rough, unforgiving countryside.

As they continued up the gravel switchback road, Nathan could tell Adelita was mesmerized by the raw beauty. Nathan loved this countryside as well. It seemed to evaporate all his stress.

After fifty-five minutes on the gravel switchback road, they arrived at the town of Bralorne, a small mining town that was abandoned in the early 1900s after workers mined over 100 million dollars in gold. Small houses dotted the mountainous valley. The mining administration building had been bought up and converted to a bed and breakfast.

Rumor had it the old hospital was haunted. Most of the abandoned homes had been bought up by vacationers, craving an escape from the rat race. The population of this historic town now stood at about 300 residents, including the part-timers. It had a bar, restaurant, hotel, and skidoo dealership. It also had a general store that served as post office, video rental, liquor, and grocery outlet.

Nathan liked the remoteness and the sparse population. Few people bothered with the gravel, sometimes impassable roads, to explore its beauty.

After driving the dangerous mountainside road they arrived at the property, stood, and surveyed the damage. Someone had vandalized the camper trailer. All the windows were smashed. Evidently an axe had been used to gouge out holes in the camper's aluminum exterior. A few items, including an axe, some cookware, camp stove, had been stolen. The outhouse had been tipped over. He felt depressed.

"Bastards," Nathan said. "Wish I could get my hands on them."

"It's okay, sweetie," Adelita assured him. "We'll clean it all up and start a fire. Relax."

She walked into the camper trailer, grabbed a broom and began sweeping up the mess. Nathan followed. He removed debris and threw it toward the fire pit, where it would eventually be burned. He was able to upright the outhouse, which pleased him.

After they finished, they sat together in lawn chairs. Nathan drank a beer and smoked. It was his seventh beer and he was well on his way to becoming pissed.

Adelita nursed hers.

Things still churned in his mind and bothered him. His financial crisis, the dreams. He hadn't dreamt much lately, at least not anything that he could remember. But he couldn't help thinking about the images, hellish and peaceful.

Inner turmoil.

Adelita approached him, knelt down, took his hand and kissed him passionately. They went into the van where they had fashioned a bed, made passionate love and drifted off to sleep.

In the early morning, Nathan was confronted by a large black bear lumbering around the campsite. There was a chill in the air, as the sun had yet to warm the mountain valley. He was in the outhouse when he first saw it. Adelita was still in the van sleeping.

He heard some twigs snap. To his left, there it was; big and black, staring with curious but friendly eyes. Nathan watched.

Bears had always fascinated him. He looked directly into its eyes, unafraid. They stared at each other for about ten seconds, but it seemed a lot longer. Then, as suddenly as the bear had stopped, it lost interest and wandered off into the bush.

An hour later, Nathan and Adelita wound their way along the winding gravel road into Gold Bridge. They were quiet, taking in the expansive mountain views, inhaling the fresh mountain air. The air was doing his hangover a world of good. Adelita gazed out the window, captivated by the beauty of their surroundings.

They arrived at the old Gold Bridge Hotel and ordered breakfast. They ate and drank coffee. "Saw a big black bear this morning," Nathan said.

She looked surprised. "You didn't say anything."

"Didn't think of it until now," he said perfunctorily. "I felt a little rough this morning."

"A little rough?" Adelita asked. "You drank enough beer to be feeling a lot rough."

"Okay, a lot rough."

They made some small-talk about the beauty of their surroundings, and then continued eating in silence. Seemed like a very peaceful silence though, not the kind where you feel you have to say something.

Despite a dull, throbbing headache, he felt relieved to be in the country. His mind wasn't quiet calm though. He thought again about the experience with Beal and the seductresses and his experience on planet Orgon.

Was it all real? Or am I losing my grip on sanity?

They left the restaurant and drove back to the acreage to spend one more night before returning to Vancouver. Nathan decided not to mention any of his dreams to Adelita. *She would definitely think I'm nuts.*

They spent a peaceful night together. Barbequed some chicken on the fire, along with some potatoes and onions that they cooked in tinfoil. Nathan only had two beers that night. Just after nine at night, he fell into Adelita's embrace and they made passionate love for two hours before falling asleep.

Chapter Fourteen

Nathan sat at Sal's, early evening on Monday. He was doing an afternoon shift because Frank had fired Scara. A customer had purchased a pack of gum and politely asked if she had change for a twenty. Her response: "Bite me," one of her all-time favorite lines. Frank's response, once the customer made him privy to this comment, "Get the fuck out of here and don't ever come back."

But there was something else on Nathan's mind tonight. He wasn't thinking of Scara. He wasn't thinking about the stalker. He wasn't thinking about the forces of good and evil. He wasn't even thinking about his massive debt load and pending foreclosure action by the bank. And he wasn't even worried that Adelita had already picked up a lot of her things from her Vancouver Island apartment and was now living with him. No, Nathan was thinking about a deal.

Immediately after arriving home, he had called Frank and convinced him to lower their asking price to $90,000. After some discussion, Frank had agreed.

Then he had called one of the suits, John. He believed he had a shot with him. He remembered the effect of the white circle. He told John they would cut Sal's loose for $90,000.

After talking to his partner, John called Nathan back, agreed to the price, and they arranged a meeting that night.

Nathan thought he could close this deal. He better close it. The phone had been ringing off the wall all day with bill collectors abusively making threats.

Although Nathan had yet to prove it to himself, he felt very adept at reading people, sorting out their motivations, and finding ways to make deals work. Well, now everything was on the line.

Or was it? *If I lose everything, can't I get it all back with the right attitude, good game plan and hard work? Even if I can't, does it matter?* He dismissed the thought quickly. *Can't think like that right now. Think of selling Sal's and getting myself out of this mess.*

Frank had left it entirely up to him to get a contract. And he had one prepared. He had written the deal with a $10,000 deposit, which would be paid directly to him; not to a lawyer in trust as is typically required. He had the balance, $80,000 due on closing, and he had the requisite buyer conditions.

He had a part-timer scheduled to come in any minute now to relieve him of his cashier duties so he could negotiate. She walked in the door. Kendra had short black hair, smart probing eyes, and an easy smile. She was good with people. She wore a black business suit, her skirt just slightly above the knees. Nathan admired her professional appearance. While he may have erred in hiring a lot of staff, he certainly hadn't with Kendra. She greeted him cheerfully.

"How's it going?"

"Good, thanks." He had briefed her on the phone and even though she knew the sale of Sal's would change her status to unemployed, she was only too happy to oblige.

"Listen," she said, approaching the cash register. "I've invited a bunch of my friends over to, you know, buy a few things to ... well ... sort of help you with negotiations."

Nathan was pleasantly surprised. "How much is this going to cost me?"

"Well, there's ten people and I've given each one of them ten dollars to spend. If you reimburse me I'll be happy."

Nathan handed her a hundred dollar bill. "Thanks a ton. You're an absolute doll."

There is something to be said for timing. And in this instance, the timing was perfect. Kendra had just prepared a fresh carafe of coffee and the suits, John and Paul, walked in the door. Nathan greeted them with a smile, grabbed his contract file and walked over to them, shaking hands.

"Glad you've come to your senses," John said. "I thought we could have inked a deal earlier, but I didn't like the asking price and I could see by what Frank was saying that you weren't prepared to drop it a whole lot."

Nathan perfunctorily nodded at the comment, introduced them to Kendra, served coffee and they sat at the bar stools in front of the storefront window. Two "customers" walked in. Their entry was not missed on the suits.

"Thank you very much for coming on such short notice," Nathan said.

"No problem," Paul jumped in. "We didn't think you were serious about selling."

"And your starting price, considering the sales, as you purport them to be, was ridiculous," John said.

"Well, the sales figures can be verified," Nathan explained. "Let's cut to the chase, shall we. The price we agreed to is $90,000. We have some conditions built into the contract for your benefit. One, verify the numbers by having one of your people spend a week here. Two, get a business license. Three, review the lease. Four, be approved by the landlord. Five, review the financials for the last two years. If you guys are okay with that the only thing we need is to review the contract, make sure it represents your interests, sign it, and cut me a check for ten thousand."

John looked confused. "You want the initial deposit to be paid to you? I thought it was supposed to go to your lawyer?"

"In this deal it goes to me," Nathan said. "We have a contract and you can de damn sure of one thing. If I am nothing else, I am a man of my word. The deposit will be deducted from your purchase price when the lawyers get the contract."

Paul looked agitated. Nathan wondered if he had been too aggressive. Paul stood. "We need some time to discuss this."

"Fair enough," Nathan replied. "If you'll notice, I left the contract open for another hour. Go ahead and take a walk if you like. Or stay here and I'll take a walk. But, just so you know, I have a few other interested parties. I have two more potential buyers coming in tomorrow afternoon. And they are dealing with the asking price of $150,000."

"You can leave," John said, with some emotion. "Give us half an hour to discuss it and we'll let you know."

"Okay," Nathan said. "I'll be over here, beside Kendra."

"Fair enough," John said.

Nathan sat beside Kendra. "I'm quite sure it's a done deal," she said, smiling.

"I hope so."

As the suits talked, Kendra's team of buyers came into the Sal's, some buying and leaving, others buying, sitting and talking.

John and Paul looked to be arguing for a few minutes, but their attention was diverted on a few occasions by the stream of customers and their lively chatter.

So we fudged a few numbers. This place is a good location. With a lot of potential. If I didn't come into this deal using other people's money, I could have made it work. As it was, he had started with zero operating capital, the number one reason coffee shops fail.

Nathan had gone in full guns blazing with no consideration of operating capital. Fundamentally the business was failing because he was borrowing from Peter to pay Paul. Leverage works sometimes. A lot of times. But seldom when you're funded by business loans at 10 percent and credit cards at 25 percent interest.

Nathan was lost in thought until he saw John's hand waving. He walked over to the waving hand. John extended it. "I think we have a deal."

Chapter Fifteen

He lay in bed the next morning contemplating the night's events. Adelita slept soundly beside him. After tying up the contract last night he was ecstatic. He closed up Sal's, arrived home at about ten-thirty, and found Adelita in bed waiting for him. He told her the news, they had a glass of wine to celebrate and spent a quiet evening together.

She stirred. He gazed at her. He was so in love. Her eyes opened. He kissed her. She kissed him back. *Nothing matters but this love.*

After making love in the shower, they sat in their bathrobes eating breakfast. Adelita had prepared *huevos mexicano*, scrambled eggs with jalapeno peppers, onions, and red peppers, colors of the Mexican flag.

Conversation was light and comical. Until the phone rang. It rang once. Twice. Three times. "Aren't you going to answer it?" Adelita finally asked.

Nathan felt a sinking feeling in his gut. We know our gut feeling doesn't often steer us wrong. It's probably ninety percent accurate. So, we tend to trust it. I mean why wouldn't we? With those averages, we only have a ten percent chance of being wrong. Even with a ten percent failure rate, it's safer to blow off everyone our gut tells us to. The ten percent that we lose, oh well; better that than distrusting our gut and getting burned.

Nathan knew answering the phone would spell trouble. But he did it anyway.

"Hello."

"Hi Nathan. It's Lena." She was sobbing on the phone. Her tone sounded almost suicidal. "How come you don't want to see me anymore?"

Nathan looked at Adelita. Her eyes narrowed. He walked into the bedroom with the phone, an action that would come to haunt him for many years to come.

"I didn't say that," Nathan said, trying to be conciliatory. "I said I would call you."

"Well you never did," Lena said, choking back tears. "All I wanted to do was be friends. After all we were together for almost three years."

Nathan felt bad. Women had a way of making him feel that way. Or maybe, it was his own shit. He didn't know. But he knew he felt bad.

Without really thinking, or perhaps without realizing that Adelita had her ear pinned to the door listening, he offered: "Take it easy, please. We can get together for coffee sometime if you like. I'll call you and we can sort it out."

Actually Nathan had said that to Lena on several occasions but had never followed up on it. He was hoping that this was just one such occasion. He hung up the phone after promising to call her.

Without warning Adelita exploded with rage. She started crying, telling Nathan he had been cheating on her, screaming and throwing things.

Ducking flying objects, Nathan tried to calm her down. "Adelita, baby, relax. I said that to get her off the line. It's only an ex-girlfriend and I have no intention of seeing her. I've told her that at least a dozen times."

"You never told me anything about her," Adelita shouted. "How the hell can I possibly trust you when you're promising to get together with your ex?" She walked around, frantically packing her things.

Nathan had to admit it didn't look good. Even though he was completely innocent, this situation was definitely worsening by the second.

Why didn't I just say I have another girlfriend and I can't talk right now? I love my new girlfriend. Something like that. Anything but the stupidity I just uttered. I must be brain-dead.

A flying glass ashtray narrowly missed his head.

In the next instant, she was walking out the door. Nathan was crushed. He tried to stop her from leaving. She shouted something unintelligible and slammed the door in his face.

He walked into the living room, collapsed on the floor, sobbing uncontrollably. He could not stop if he wanted to. His emotions had reached a boiling point. He sat on the carpet and cried. He was in shock. He was so in love with Adelita. And now she was gone. Gone, because he, who fancied himself such a shrewd negotiator, had picked up the phone and talked like a complete imbecile to his ex-girlfriend.

He curled up on the carpet sobbing until the wee hours of the morning.

Chapter Sixteen

In his dream, he was in bed with Adelita wrapped in a tight embrace. They had just finished making love and he felt exhausted but very satisfied. He felt a sensation of sandpaper on his cheek and woke to Matty licking his face. The realization of what had happened the night before sank in and he felt overcome by sadness again.

He stroked Matty gently, and she started purring immediately, kneading his chest with her paws. Matty seemed to sense something tragic had happened and she comforted him.

He heard banging at the door. Nathan thought it was inside his head initially but then realized someone was actually knocking at the door. He lifted Matty off his chest and approached the door, squinting through the peephole. Blue uniforms. One male, one female. *Cops. Shit!*

"Who, is it?" he asked, even though he knew.

"It's the police," said the male voice. "Could you open the door? We'd like to ask you some questions."

Nathan opened the door. Young male cop, in his early thirties with short, neatly cropped black hair. And well-trimmed mustache. Mustache wore an expression of curiosity. Female cop, probably late fifties, age lines creasing her weathered face. She wasn't aging gracefully. Her eyes drilled into him with an expression of disgust. Disgust spoke first.

"You been assaulting women," she said, more of a statement than a question.

"Can I see your identification, please?" Nathan asked, stalling, trying to think of something that wouldn't incriminate him. You had to be careful with cops.

They produced their badges. He eyed them closely.

"A woman named Adelita showed up last night at a shelter for battered women. Tells us you've been beating her," Disgust said, glaring at him scornfully. Nathan knew that for women to be accepted into such places they had to tell stories of abusive spouses.

"I don't know what you're talking about," he said, rubbing sleep from his eyes. "We had an argument. She started throwing things at me, and stormed out the door."

"That's bullshit, and we both know it," Disgust insisted. Mustache didn't look so sure. It seemed he wanted to hear Nathan's side of the story before jumping to conclusions.

"Did you see any marks on her?" Nathan asked. "Surely, if I beat her up you would see some evidence of it, wouldn't you?"

Disgust hesitated.

"I didn't notice any marks," Mustache said.

"There doesn't necessarily have to be marks to prove you beat her," Disgust explained. "You slapped her in the face several times, didn't you? You better come clean now or it's gonna be worse for you later."

"I have no idea what you're talking about," Nathan said. "And I believe I've had enough of this conversation. If you're trying to convict me solely based on what Adelita is telling you, without any regard for my side of the story, maybe I need to talk to a lawyer."

"That won't be necessary," said Mustache. He seemed to believe what Nathan was saying. "All we're doing here is investigating a complaint. When we get a call from the women's shelter on these matters, we have to follow up."

Disgust was ready to explode. She bit her tongue and remained silent while Mustache continued. "Adelita told us she wishes to collect her belongings tonight. She wants a police escort to access your apartment."

Nathan thought about this. It seemed she hated him so much that she was prepared to concoct any story to exact her revenge. What would she do to his apartment if he let her in? Plant some damning evidence? He didn't know what she was capable of.

But he certainly didn't trust her anymore.

"Here's how it's gonna work," he said, thinking that he would have the locks changed as soon as the cops left. "I'll pack up her belongings. There isn't much here. And I'll leave them out on the balcony at eight. I'll watch for a police car, assuming you'll be driving her here. And when I see one, I'll leave and she can help herself to her stuff." After a moment's thought: "If I'm not here one of my friends will be."

The cops considered this for a moment. "Fine," Disgust said. "Whatever you do, don't leave town. If I find even the slightest scratch on Adelita, I'll be back. And it won't be pretty."

Nathan returned her nasty stare. Mustache looked down at his hands. Breathing deeply, Nathan shut the door. He hoped nothing further would come of Adelita's fictitious complaint.

Chapter Seventeen

Nathan spent the day working and taking care of domestic chores. He had the locks changed. Life must go on. It was five in the afternoon and he was on his way to Santo's, a tapas bar on Commercial Drive, and one of his favorite haunts.

He had deposited the suits' check in the bank to cover overdue rent. Sal's would breathe another day. He had met with Frank, dropped the purchase contract off at his lawyer's, popped in to see Kendra and her friends, who were making it look as busy as a Safeway supermarket on Christmas Eve.

He even paid some of the minimum balances on his credit cards and the mortgage arrears on his condo. He still felt bad about Adelita's departure but the visit by the cops had scared the shit out of him. Now his sadness was mixed with feelings of distrust and fear. He thought about his relationship with Adelita and realized he should have taken things much slower. Having her move in so early, particularly when he had so many problems, was a bad idea.

He remembered shortly after Adelita moved in being awakened in the middle of the night to wracking sobs coming from the bathroom. Frightened, he had jumped out of the bed quickly, knocked on the door and called out her name. When no one answered, he had finally opened the door to find her in a fetal position in the shower, hot water cascading off her naked body.

She was sobbing uncontrollably. He had comforted her and brought her to bed, assuming whatever was bothering her they could discuss later. With all the other shit in his life, he hadn't followed up on that episode to find out what was wrong.

Fetal position. Reminds me of someone else I know. Don't think about that. I'm too afraid to think about it.

It was fear that motivated him now to try and get his life in order. He still had a lot of other things on his mind. He wondered if the white circle on his palm led to the suits inking the conditional deal on Sal's. And he worried the cops would be paying him another visit.

He thought maybe some fajitas and sangria might fix him up.

He had talked to his friend Michelle earlier in the day, left a new key for her, and she was at his apartment now, packing Adelita's belongings in plastic garbage bags and putting them out on the balcony.

He walked into Santo's. It was dimly lit. Salsa music played. He wasn't surprised to see his friend Dave sitting at the bar, flirting with the bartender, a rather stunning black-haired beauty.

"How are you, buddy?"

"I'm still alive," Nathan responded, pulling up a bar stool beside him. Black-haired Beauty smiled at Nathan and he mustered a half smile. He ordered a pitcher of sangria and some fajitas.

"Been seeing any aliens lately? Hey your face is full of white circles. What's with that?" Dave asked.

"Please, I'm not exactly in the mood for jokes right now." He explained some of his good news, that he had a conditional sale on Sal's, and some of his bad, that Adelita had moved out. He omitted the story about the cops. Couldn't bother to regurgitate the whole mess.

"Doesn't sound like things are that bad," Dave assured him. "Lots of fish in the sea."

Dave was one of those guys who couldn't commit to a woman. He had to have them all. Or at least try to. He was very successful in business, however, if not in relationships. He had successfully built and sold three very large condominium projects and had to be worth at least five million by now. He measured his happiness by the amount of money he could accumulate. And viewed women as nothing more than objects to be conquered and then discarded.

Nathan wasn't one to wallow in his own self-pity. And he didn't even want to talk about anything serious right now. He felt a void in his heart and in his mind but thought enough sangria would fix that. *What the hell it's Friday after all, and I'm taking tomorrow off.*

He wanted some time alone tomorrow, to reflect on what had happened to him lately and how his own bad judgment had contributed to his emotional and financial mess. And he was far from out of the woods now, with credit card bills still mounting, the threat of the cops returning, and the possibility the deal on Sal's would collapse.

"You're absolutely right," Nathan said. "Cheers to sex without emotion."

"I'll drink to that," and they clinked glasses.

Dave flirted with Black-haired Beauty, who eventually introduced herself as Mary Sol.

Nathan finished his fajitas, was on his fourth glass of sangria and beginning to feel the lazy, comforting buzz of wine.

He chatted with Dave and they exchanged flirtatious comments with Mary Sol. Nathan was surprised at his own good humor the night after Adelita had dumped him. *Could have been the cop visit. Made me re-examine the whole thing in a different light. Then again, maybe it was the sangria.*

He glanced around Santo's as Dave chatted with Mary Sol. He noticed someone looking at him who seemed strangely familiar. The man sat with two attractive and sexily dressed women, who lavished attention on him. They laughed and drank and were completely enthralled with his banter.

Shit, that's Beal. He got Dave's attention and noticed Beal look over as he did. "Don't look over right away, but see that man at the table with those women? He's the man in my dream. It's Beal." Dave had an alcohol buzz going and he grinned. In a moment, he looked where Nathan had pointed.

"Go up and say hi," Dave said. "Tell him you know him from somewhere."

He glanced at Beal's table again. Now he also recognized the two women. He had made love with both of them that night. Now, one of them smiled teasingly and gave him a wink. He was convinced. It took about five minutes for Nathan to muster the courage to approach the table. His curiosity got the better of him.

"Excuse me," he said, approaching. "But do I know you from somewhere?"

The lively chatter stopped. "Come to think of it, I believe we did meet somewhere before," Beal said. "At a party, I think, but I can't remember which one."

Nathan tried to remember a party where he might have met Beal. Nothing came to mind.

"You're right, I remember now. Last year. A party. The north shore. A friend of Michelle's, if I remember correctly. You know Michelle, right?" Beal asked.

"Good friend of mine," Nathan said, but still couldn't remember meeting Beal there. He searched his mind to no avail.

"I think the party was at ... Mike's house—that's his name," Beal said.

Nathan knew Mike. He lived with his girlfriend in a nice house on the north shore with a beautiful city view. Somewhere off Mountain Highway. He remembered going to Mike's house party last year but couldn't remember Beal. He did, however, remember that he was very drunk at the time. He could always confirm it with Michelle.

"Right," Nathan said. "I remember the party now. And I believe I remember you there," he lied. "So you know Michelle?"

"Only in passing. But, yes."

"Are you Beal?"

"Excellent memory," Beal said. "And you're Ethan right?"

"Nathan," he corrected. "But that's close enough. I've been called a hell of a lot worse." *Is that a Freudian slip?*

Beal laughed, introduced his female friends as Tamara and Cassandra. They smiled knowingly and Tamara offered him a seat. "Join us, please. Invite your friend over if you like."

Nathan considered. He had to admit he was afraid of this man, but at the same time drawn to his lascivious lifestyle. He looked at his watch. It was already well past ten. He was about to respond when his cell phone rang, giving him time to think. "Excuse me, please," he said, stepping out of earshot.

He recognized the number as Michelle's. "Hey," he said. "How did everything go over there?"

"It's all good. There's a police van pulling away right now, with her and her stuff."

"Great. Thanks a ton, Michelle. I owe you big-time. I'm heading home shortly. You can hang onto the key if you like. I have a spare." He noticed Beal watching him with a grin as he talked on the phone. The women at his table chatted and laughed.

Dave was engrossed in conversation with Mary Sol. Nathan thought about inviting Michelle to Santo's, a short distance away from his apartment, but thought better of it. If he was going to get sucked into Beal's lifestyle, he certainly wasn't about to drag his friends down with him.

At least not now anyway.

"I'll be gone by the time you get here," Michelle said. Good, she already had plans. "I have to meet Stephen."

"Okay, I have to go. Thanks again. I'll call you later. There's something I need to ask you about."

He hung up and approached Dave. Mary Sol was serving drinks. "Is it the devil incarnate?" Dave asked, grinning drunkenly.

"I don't feel good about that guy. He invited us over but I don't think it's a good idea."

Dave was making good progress with Mary Sol. Nathan hoped that would keep him distracted.

"Is it the guy in your dream?" Dave asked.

"Yes," Nathan said gravely.

"Well aren't you at least going to introduce me?" Dave asked, his gaze lingering on the babes seated at Beal's table.

"No," Nathan said. "Listen, I'm going home. I'll talk to you later."

Nathan walked back to the table. He didn't know why he was giving Beal the courtesy of telling him he was leaving.

"I hope everything is okay on the home front," Beal said.

Odd that he would ask such a question. "Yeah, it was just a friend. Listen, thanks a lot for the invite, but I should be going now. Had a late night and need to get some sleep."

Beal grinned. "No problem. Listen I'm having a party at my home in the British Properties next Saturday. If you want to come you're welcome. Bring a few friends if you like." He handed Nathan a card.

"Thanks. I'll think about it," Nathan said, returning to the bar.

"I'm leaving," Nathan said. "Do you want to come over for a beer?" He said this more out of fear that Dave would get connected with Beal rather than a need for any company. He remembered Beal's threats in his dream and now they resonated with a realness he didn't care to think about.

"No thanks, buddy. Maybe I'll see you on the weekend. I'm this close to getting a date with Mary Sol."

Before leaving, Nathan made Dave promise he would have nothing to do with Beal's table. Dave thought Nathan had lost his mind, but gave him his word.

Chapter Eighteen

"You remember Mike," Michelle said, over coffee at Joe's Cappuccino Bar. "We played beach volleyball with him a few years back." Nathan thought about it. It was Saturday morning and the first thing he did when he woke up was try to reach Adelita. He wanted to apologize to her and try and make things right again. He had called the nearest woman's shelter but the woman on the phone would not confirm or deny if Adelita was there.

In any event, she had said, the shelter's policy was to not allow communication between the clients and their exes. They did not promote reconciliations after abuse.

The second call was to Michelle and she had agreed to meet at Joe's. They sat and talked.

"Oh yeah," Nathan said after a long pause. "I do remember Mike. Big guy, renovator, drank a lot. What about Beal? Do you know him?"

Michelle said she remembered meeting him at Mike's party and he had at least two trophy girls hanging off him. He wasn't her friend, however. In fact, he gave her the creeps. But, she thought, he might be a friend of Mike's.

"I don't remember Beal at the party," Nathan said.

"You were quite wasted. I'm surprised you even remember the party."

He remembered the party, but only vaguely. He remembered having a blow-out on that day with Lena and she had angrily hung up on him. By the time he had arrived, he was three quarters in the bag. He didn't remember leaving or how he got there, but had vague memories of enjoying the city view through an alcoholic fog.

"Something else sticks in my mind about that party," Michelle said, "But it's probably just coincidence or something."

"What?"

Michelle didn't want to freak Nathan out. She knew he had gone through two break-ups in a very short amount of time, and was still struggling to get out of a financial crisis. And she thought his drinking lately was getting way out of hand. Sometimes he didn't make a lot of sense.

"What's this all about anyway?" she asked, trying to shift the conversation. Nathan explained his dreams and finished by saying Beal wanted his soul in exchange for money, power, and all the women he could handle.

He produced his palm but the circle was hardly visible. She looked at it but didn't seem convinced of anything.

Michelle wasn't sure how secure Nathan's grip on reality was at that moment. He looked rough. *But, hell,* she thought, *he's been through a lot lately and who wouldn't be a bit off the wall.*

He still seemed to be functioning and had managed to put a contract together on the sale of Sal's. *He must have some neurons still firing properly. Maybe I should tell him?* she thought. If she didn't, she feared someone else would get hurt.

"Well, I doubt you remember, but Mike's father Andy was at the party." Nathan shook his head. "I didn't think you would. Anyway, I saw Andy talking to Beal for a while out on the deck. Andy looked upset about something. A little while later he left."

Nathan dreaded where the story was going. "And?"

"Didn't you hear? He committed suicide the next night. Jumped off the eighth floor of a high-rise."

Nathan's face turned white. He thought he was going to be sick. Michelle touched his arm. "Are you okay?"

He took a few deep breaths and tried to focus on the streetwalkers passing by and the sunshine that was beginning to warm him. He reached for a cigarette. Lately he had switched to DuMaurier Distinct, a cigarette much smoother than the cigars. Michelle offered him a light as his hands jittered holding the smoke. He took it and she lit a cigarette as well. They smoked for a while in silence.

Finally, Nathan said. "Beal told me it would spell my demise if I didn't accept his offer. Maybe the same thing happened to Andy?"

"Who knows?" Michelle said. But her gut told her something was wrong.

"Have you talked to Mike lately?" Nathan asked.

"Not for a long time. I went to the funeral. He was real messed up about it."

"Well, maybe one of us should call him, see how he's doing. You know him better than I do. Could you do it?"

"Sure. I'll call him later."

Nathan told her about the upcoming party Beal had invited him to. After thinking about it, he wanted to go, if only to try and prevent any more deaths.

Michelle said she wanted to attend. She was always up for adventure. She could bring her boyfriend Stephen, who definitely had a dark side. A self-described atheist, Stephen was the kind of guy who would get a thrill out of anything that had to do with devil worship.

Although Nathan was good friends with Stephen, he wasn't sure it was a good idea for either of them to attend. *Why did I even tell her?*

"It could be dangerous. I wouldn't advise it," he said.

Michelle wasn't listening to his protests. "How could I live with myself if I didn't go and something happened to you—knowing that maybe I could have stopped it?"

Nathan knew she wouldn't take no for an answer. He gave up the address and they agreed to go together in the same vehicle.

He hugged her tightly and they parted company.

Chapter Nineteen

Nathan sat on a white bench overlooking a pastoral river view. White mushroom-shaped buildings and lush green rolling hills dotted the landscape.

Very few sounds could be heard but for the faint whirring of the air gliders buzzing by on the air highway behind him. Birds also chirped in the distance, and Nathan could hear the gurgling sound of a babbling brook. He assumed he was dreaming but he didn't want to disrupt the feeling of peace and tranquility.

His hand felt warm. He noticed it was joined with a petite blonde-haired woman dressed in a flowing white gown. She was slim with small and very plain features. But she possessed a calmness and inner beauty. He had felt the same feeling in his other dream, but this woman looked much different. Oh, she still had the stunning green eyes, but her facial features were more distinct; small nose, mouth, ears, but very large eyes. Her skin was as white as snow.

Nathan welcomed the euphoric feeling that streamed through his body, while he held her hand. He also knew if he was going to be any match for Beal, he needed to have the white circle back. *Maybe I can get it here?*

"How are you, Nathan?" the woman asked.

"I'm fine." He looked into her green eyes, eyes that possessed such beauty, radiance and warmth. "And you?"

"I'm Ophelia, the daughter of Orb, the leader of planet Orgon. As you remember, you have been here before. You met Orb. He made you an offer to live here for seven years, teach you the ways of our culture, so you can spread these teachings on Earth."

Nathan was more receptive this time. The way he saw it, he had a very real problem. He felt absolutely certain his life and the lives of his friends were in danger.

To choose not to subscribe to Beal's way of life meant death. Of that, Nathan felt certain. And Beal wanted to cut a swath of destruction through Earth by corrupting everyone he could. And there was that suicide with Mike's father, Andy. *And what about Mike?* Nathan had an odd feeling something was wrong there.

And Dave. Had he ignored his warning to steer clear of Beal? There was a good chance he hadn't. But how can I stop Beal?

The pleasurable sensations Ophelia was sending him snapped him from his worries. He thought she said something. "Sorry, did you say something?"

"My father—he wants to see you after we have lunch."

"Okay," Nathan agreed, "I'll see him again." He looked at Ophelia's eyes and saw nothing but pure, unconditional love. He wanted to kiss her. *What the fuck am I doing, transitioning from one relationship to another? I thought I could be satisfied with my own company? I must be really fucked up.*

"I have a lot of questions," Nathan said. "And a few problems I need to take care of on Earth before I can do anything."

"We know of your problems," Ophelia said. "But, please, tell me what's on your mind."

"In one of my nightmares, I met this evil guy, Beal. Anyway, he wants me to sell my soul for a life of lasciviousness or he'll kill me."

"And you don't want the kind of lifestyle he's offering?"

"No, I've tried it on my own and it isn't working."

There was a momentary pause. "What else?" Ophelia asked.

"I know what Orb wants. But, if I'm going to stay here for a while, I need to be sure my friends on Earth are protected."

"We might be able to help you with that," she said.

"How?"

"Come and see Orb and he'll explain."

Nathan stared at her, confused.

"Something else?" Ophelia asked.

"Yeah, why me?"

"Nathan, the reason my father picked you is because of the way you have been living; in solitude, drinking a lot, a disdain for people, a reckless pursuit of material gain at the expense of others. You're a prime candidate for reformation."

"You mean I need to be taught a lesson?"

Ophelia continued without acknowledging the question. "As for Beal, we've known about him for a long time. His power only works on the weak. If you live in a morally correct fashion, it doesn't work. Think of when he approached you—when you were at your weakest point emotionally."

"I suppose that's true," Nathan said. "But can we get rid of Beal permanently?"

"All we can do is introduce a new way of thinking that centers around love, caring for others, helping others and respect for the environment and animals. If that succeeds, we can keep evil at bay to prolong the life of Earth and its inhabitants."

"But evil will always be there lurking," Nathan said.

"If people live their lives in a morally upright fashion, evil cannot take root. But your planet is in chaos now. Murder rates up. Reckless destruction of your planet. Racial discrimination. Robberies. Corruption. Meaningless wars. The inequality created by capitalism. The list goes on. At this rate, your race only has another fifty years left before it will self-destruct. As a peaceful planet, we look at this as an opportunity to right this destructive course of action, prolong the life of Earth and its inhabitants, minimize the impact of the corruptive forces."

There was another long pause. "How do I deal with Beal if my weak state makes me susceptible to his power?"

"Not everything at once." Ophelia tugged at his arm. "Walk with me through the garden for a few minutes."

They stood up and she kissed him on the cheek. It caused a warm, pulsing sensation to reverberate through his body. He loved that feeling. If these people, interacted in this fashion, no wonder they didn't experience the likes of evil.

As they walked he wondered about a lot of things. How they made their money? What they did for excitement? Did they have any bars, any good drugs? Maybe he wouldn't be able to handle things here? Too much for him. Too much of a culture shock. And what of his relationship failures of late? Didn't seem much good at that.

He had his doubts.

Ophelia seemed to read his thoughts, but his expression was probably a dead giveaway anyway. She pulled him closer, putting her arm around him. He felt better.

How many times have I thought that?

He sat across from her at the kitchen table and ate a bowl of green stuff. While it looked like puke, it tasted rather good.

No more burgers here. He drank a thick brownish juice that revitalized him.

Her dome-shaped house was painted in designer green tones and furnished with plush black leather-like chairs. The high-tech kitchen was open to the rest of the home and featured a variety of buttons and cooking appliances. Nathan had no idea what to make of them. In the living room there was a large screen on a wall and a large bay window that provided a soothing view to a lush green landscape.

Nathan had expected something hospital white and sterile but it was quite the opposite.

He took a drink of the pasty juice. "Have I actually left my apartment now, or am I only here in spirit, or something?"

"Oh, no, you're here all right," Ophelia said. "Our spaceship brought you here. Explanations will come later, if you really want to know."

"What about us? Why am I here with you … and, I don't mean to be presumptuous, but are we supposed to be a couple?"

"Do you like that idea?" Ophelia asked, her features brightening.

Nathan just stared at her. It was a little premature to answer right now.

"My father has been watching your life for many years, through the orb-finder lens. And, he's been grooming me to be with you. I've known about your arrival for some time and have been anxiously waiting."

Spontaneously Ophelia sprang up and started dancing around the kitchen with a robot device that had whirred into the room. About three feet tall with a silvery metal finish, the robot had big blue eyes that looked more real than mechanical. It was dressed in a white apron and matching white hat. Ophelia introduced it as Maiden.

Nathan couldn't help laughing at the sight of his new mate dancing with a mechanical robot in a futuristic house on planet Orgon.

Maiden spoke in a mechanical voice. "Clean now, or dance?"

Ophelia released the robot. "Go ahead and clean. I'm just so happy I'm finally here with Nathan." Maiden went to work cleaning the kitchen.

Ophelia took him by the arm. "Come, we must speak to Orb now. We have to tell him of your plans to join us."

"Did I say that?"

In the living room, the large screen fluttered to life. Black slowly became white. The camera, or so it seemed, led them up the winding stairs to the top of a plateau. Orb, his white head and green eyes barely visible through the mist, sat on an ornate throne.

"Welcome Nathan. I'm glad you've met my daughter and had the chance to become acquainted with Orgon. What do you think?" he asked.

"It's interesting, I'll say that much."

"Will you leave your planet, live with us for seven years, bring back our pearls of wisdom to Earth and communicate them to your people?"

"I can't promise anything like that right now. But if you're willing to help me with the Beal problem on Earth, I will promise you this; I will stay for three months, see if I can adjust to your customs, culture, way of life, and I'll make my decision from there."

"The Beal problem, as you put it, has been around for centuries, and has become ingrained in the human consciousness. Our best minds have given it a lot of thought. At best, we can tame his influence to a manageable level. If he senses any human weakness, he is able to corrupt a mind fully. To keep evil at a manageable level we must introduce a new way of thinking, a more positive and morally upright way of living for you Earthlings."

"Well, all I want to do is make sure my friends are out of harm's way, before I can even commit to three months. You have to understand a few things. I'm a human being, completely unaccustomed to your ways. I need time to see if I can handle it. Maybe I spend a week here and decide I want to stay that self-serving capitalist pig with a skewed value system," Nathan said.

Ophelia put her hand on his knee. He felt a warm sensation overwhelm his body. He looked in her eyes, so intensely sincere, a look he had never seen before.

"I promise you Nathan, you will experience true love and happiness on Orgon. Loyalty and devotion the likes of which perhaps cannot be experienced on Earth," Orb said.

Nathan had much to learn about the Orgon culture. He knew he could use a cold beer and a smoke right about now but didn't dare ask about the permissibility of such vices on Orgon.

Not right away, anyway.

"This is what we are prepared to do," Orb continued. "We'll send you back to Earth with the power to help you deal with Beal. Warn him there is a new way of thinking that will soon mitigate his evil powers. These words should distract him from his current path of destruction, and focus more on the recruits he already has, solidifying his alliance with them, instead of rampantly recruiting more, as he is doing now. Go to the party. Try and save your friends—if they indeed want to be saved. Then stay with us three months. At the end of three months, we'll revisit this issue. Do you agree?"

There was a short pause.

"Yes," Nathan said. He was about to add something else but the screen faded to black. And, now he couldn't remember what it was anyway.

He spent the day touring the city with Ophelia in an air glider and asking questions. He wanted to learn as much as he could. They didn't have jobs for money. They worked for credits which could buy them various essentials. Each citizen was given a house and enough land to have a self-sustaining farm. They were vegetarians, for the most part, but got their protein from fish. Education and health care were provided free by the government that Orb headed.

Nuclear energy fueled the gliders, powered their homes and ran almost everything. They generated some electricity from the water sources. The climate was warm all year round, only dipping slightly in the winter. It was also lush and green with many lakes and rivers and a large ocean, from which they harvested fish.

Since there was no disparity between the rich and the poor, they were all essentially equal in their material possessions. They had no reason to compete. There was no point to it. They didn't chase money just for the sake of it. Materialism didn't mean anything to Orgonions, as they had everything they needed.

The relationships they formed could by agreement not be mutually exclusive. These contracts would be negotiated at the outset to determine how long the parties wanted to stay together. Typically, a contract would last for seven years after which the parties would have the option of renewing the contract or not. And the contracts would specify the nature of the relationship, whether infidelity was permitted, or if it was a liaison strictly for child rearing.

Nathan learned Orgon had two hundred settlements. Venice, where he was now, had a population of about 100,000. Orgon also had liaisons with three other distant, inhabited planets: Urellian, Pluton, and Necruse.

Amongst all the white gliders, Nathan spotted a few black ones. "What are they for," he asked as Ophelia expertly navigated the air highways. "Oh, they're the watchmen," she explained.

"What like policeman?"

"Sort of but they don't carry guns. There's no need. We haven't had a murder here in over 80 years, and that was when we were invaded by the Urellians. It wasn't murder, really. It was war. We were defending our planet."

"How do you know you won't be invaded again?"

"We have a peace pact. You see, Orgon is one of the few sources of uranium and plutonian, used to manufacture nuclear power. We all have to work the uranium mines at least three months of the year to keep our planet functioning. We also supply Urellians with uranium and plutonium and they navigate the perimeter of our sky-sphere and protect us from potential invasive forces. We also have a nuclear bomb, aimed at their planet that can be detonated in an instant. You know, mutual nuclear deterrence, like détente on Earth."

Peace based on the threat of imminent danger. They get along because of that bomb. He was sure the Urellians had one trained on Orgon as well.

"What about Necruse and Pluton?" Nathan asked. "Don't you need a nuclear bomb trained on those planets as well?"

"Not really. Pluton is aligned with Orgon and doesn't have any military capability. Necruse, aligned with Urellian, also has a limited army. We have a formidable military capability because we are the only planet that has the uranium and plutonium used to manufacture nuclear energy which our trade partners rely on us for. Since we have been attacked for our resources in the past, we have learned from these experiences and prepared for the unlikely possibility that we may be invaded."

Seems like a rather fragile alliance, Nathan thought. But, he supposed, it was not all that unlike the alliances on Earth.

Nathan knew there was a lot more to learn here. But he was beginning to see how they had fashioned a peaceful existence for themselves. Mankind could learn a lot from their example.

But the fragility of the alliance nagged at him.

Chapter Twenty

"Dead? What do you mean dead?" Nathan asked.

He was on the phone with Michelle. He had been transported back to Earth. It was Monday. He had lost almost two full days on Orgon. He was just waking up when he heard the phone ringing and groggily answered it.

"I called a few times. Where were you?"

He paused. "Decided to take a trip to the acreage, chill a bit." He hoped the answer would satisfy her.

"I mean committed suicide, six months to the day. I talked to Renata. She's on medication for depression."

Nathan thought about it. Both of them had been in contact with Beal at Mike's party. Mike's father, Andy had committed suicide. Now Mike. This sounded way too much like a coincidence. And Nathan didn't believe in coincidences anymore.

"This sounds pretty messed up," he said.

"I know," Michelle said. "Listen, I have to run. We still on for Beal's party?"

"Yeah. Could we meet for coffee before that?"

She agreed and hung up.

Nathan looked at the clock. Just before noon. Before checking his answering machine, he had to call Dave. He dialed the number.

"Yeah?" Dave answered groggily.

"How's it going?"

"Oh, hey Nathan, okay. Actually a little hungover. What happened to you Saturday? I called about tennis and never heard back."

"Sorry, a little tied up. What happened Friday night at Santo's? Tell me you didn't go near Beal, or any of his women."

"Actually, Mary Sol told me she had a boyfriend. Bitch led me on half the night before telling me that. I partied with Beal Friday night. I brought Tamara back to my apartment. She's a wild one in the sack. Like nothing I've ever experienced."

He noticed Dave's tone sounded more sinister than usual. Could be the hangover, but he thought he detected an edge to his voice.

"Listen, you could be in danger," Nathan said. "I'd like to meet you for coffee later this week to discuss a few things. Michelle and Stephen will be there as well."

"Sure, no problem, call me. I can't wait for Beal's party this weekend."

"We'll talk Wednesday," Nathan said. "Try and stay out of trouble." He hung up the phone, wondering how a guy like Dave could possibly resist any sort of temptation. Dave was way worse than Nathan when it came to that.

Nathan headed for Sal's. Frank had left three messages, the last one delivered in a rude tone. The suits wanted to meet at Sal's tonight to discuss the contract. Nathan had called Frank and he didn't sound at all impressed. The only excuse Nathan could think of was that he was rattled by Adelita's departure and had spent the weekend in Bralorne without his phone.

"Well, make damn sure you show up tonight," Frank had said, slamming the receiver down.

Later that night, Nathan, Frank, John and Paul sat at a round table inside Sal's sipping coffee. Kendra worked the cash register. A man stood beside her, keeping track of sales. His presence was one of the suits' conditions; that they have someone at Sal's for a few weeks to verify the numbers. Customers came and went. Nathan recognized a few of Kendra's friends in the mix. He suspected Frank was paying them off.

Outside it was a gray, drizzly day.

The suits had verified the financials, been approved by the landlord, obtained a business license, reviewed the lease. The only other condition had to do with their man spending another week or so in Sal's.

"I think we're prepared to sign off on all the conditions," John said. "Let the lawyers handle the rest."

Nathan tried to hide his elation. He was about to speak, but Frank jumped in.

"Congratulations gentlemen on being the new owners of Sal's. I know you'll find this location has excellent potential." Frank stood and heartily shook the suits' hands.

Nathan stood and did the same. He explained to the suits that he had injured his right hand while playing tennis so he had to use his left. Actually, after returning from Orgon, he had noticed the white circle had reappeared on his palm, glowing brighter than ever. He was afraid it would lose its power if he used it to shake hands.

He produced the paperwork and the suits signed off on all conditions, making it a done deal. The suits left the building.

"Good job," Frank said, and offered a handshake.

"Thanks," he said. They talked small-talk for a while and Frank asked Nathan if he wanted to be partners on a new Sal's.

"Listen," Nathan said, "the money I get from this deal won't be enough to cover debts on Sal's or my personal debts. I'll be starting from nothing, without a pot to piss in. The farthest thing from my mind is doing another business. Even if I wanted to, I don't have the money or borrowing power to even think about it."

He would shut the magazine distribution business down, put the condo up for sale, probably at a loss, and try to negotiate a deal with his creditors in the hope of salvaging what remained of his dismal credit rating. Either way he looked at it, financially he was in ruins. *At least there's nowhere else to go but up*. His financial situation couldn't get much worse.

"Well anyway, keep it in mind if your situation improves," Frank said, and left.

Chapter Twenty-One

It was a sunny Wednesday. Nathan, Michelle, Stephen and Dave sat patio-side at Joe's Cappuccino bar, sipping their coffees and smoking cigarettes. Tuesday had been a busy day for Nathan. He had met with his accountant to straighten out his taxes, his lawyer, who had negotiated a settlement with the creditors; fifteen cents on the dollar or nothing at all. They had all been called individually as well as notified in writing of Nathan's dismal financial situation. What they were told was simply this; accept fifteen cents on the dollar or Nathan declares bankruptcy and you get nothing.

Letters and phone calls had also gone out to creditors of Sal's and Frank steadfastly maintained he would not share in any of that debt. His view: "The store was under your management, you eat it."

While Nathan viewed this as hardly fair since they were equal partners in the business, he also knew Frank wouldn't budge on his position.

In any event, he had converted $60,000 in coffee shop debt to $9,000 and $50,000 of personal debt to $7,500. He figured if all it cost him was $16,500 to be rid of the friendship, it was money well spent.

He had also listed his east Vancouver one bedroom condo for $239,900. At that price he would be taking at least a $20,000 hit, but the market had dropped and he felt now was the time to make a fresh start.

"Hey, wake up and smell the coffee, buddy," Dave said. "What's on your mind?" Nathan had been lost in thought while the others talked.

Nathan outlined his concerns to his friends and reiterated that Mike and Andy were both dead after their encounter with Beal. He also told them about his plans to leave soon for planet Orgon to spend three months with Ophelia.

"Nathan, buddy, I've known you a long time and never known you to be a bullshitter but this stuff sounds wacked, dude. And keep your voice down. We don't want our neighbors here to think you've been let out for the weekend," Stephen said.

Stephen was like that. He always spoke his mind, like it or not. The word discretion was not part of his vocabulary.

"Take a look at this," Nathan said, deciding to cut to the chase. He exposed his right palm. They stared at the glowing white circle.

Stephen grabbed Nathan's hand, tried to rub off the circle. "You been painting, or whaa ..."

Suddenly he withdrew his hand, and his demeanor changed noticeably. He was beaming.

"Wow, do I feel good," Stephen said. "That some kind of drug or something?"

"What's going on?" Michelle asked.

"What's with the circle?" Dave asked.

"You can see for yourself. And you can see the affect it has on people. I got it on Orgon. Orb gave it to me to help neutralize Beal."

Stephen complimented Michelle on how beautiful she looked and leaned over to kiss her.

While a little surprised, she was happy for the affection and reciprocated.

"I don't get it," Dave said. "Let's say we go along with everything, and it seems you have some pretty fucking strong evidence here ... what exactly do you want from us? What do you want us to do at this party?"

"I don't get all of it either," Nathan said. "And I don't really know what to say to you except be careful. Maybe you shouldn't come, none of you. This started off as my problem, and I should be the one finishing it, without putting your lives at risk."

But they wouldn't hear his argument. They agreed if Nathan was in trouble then they all wanted to be there to try and protect him. Nathan gave up on the argument, but also wondered how he was supposed to save them if he was leading them willingly into the devil's snare.

"Michelle, I want to give you power of attorney over my affairs while I'm gone. I'll pay you. I'll give you all the details later. It includes taking Matty. Are you okay with that?"

"Sure," she said, wondering if he would really leave them.

Chapter Twenty-Two

Saturday night. They drove in Nathan's van up the winding road that led to Beal's home, a 20,000 square-foot stone mansion with outbuildings that included maid's quarters, large gazebo and six-car garage. The estate home was well located on a treed and manicured ten-acre property that offered panoramic ocean and city views. A circular driveway led to the main entrance, where a water fountain displayed a grey statue of an alluring woman, posing seductively on a pedestal, cascading water splashing over her nakedness. She cupped a well-formed breast in one hand, while her other hand massaged her thigh. She smiled toward the house.

Expensive cars were parked everywhere. Pulling into the driveway, Nathan was met by a clean-cut man in a black suit, who offered to park his vehicle. He surrendered the keys and they stepped out and walked up the large staircase to the house. Nathan noticed a large, glass-enclosed swimming pool to his left, naked people dancing around the patio, drinks in hand, and more naked people swimming. Even from outside, he could see that part of the pool disappeared out of sight, winding its way into a cavernous grotto area of the property. Although he had never been to Hugh Hefner's mansion, he imagined this is what it would be like.

"Please, try and stay together," Nathan said, as they entered. "And be careful what you wish for."

Inside, the mansion buzzed with activity. Waiters served drinks and appetizers. People laughed and talked. Black Sabbath cranked out *Ironman* from a stereo. People danced, some in various stages of undress. It was a wild party. The home was tastefully decorated with antique furniture, oak walls and expensive art.

The four stood together, drinks in hand, made comments about the party, people watched. Beal approached. "Here he comes," Nathan said and the conversation stopped abruptly.

"Glad you could all make it," Beal said, and began shaking hands, starting with Dave. "Good to see you, my friend. Tamara's in the pool, if you decide you want a swim. There's also a large hot tub in the back grotto for your pleasure."

To Michelle and Stephen, shaking their hands: "Nice to see you again. We met at a party last year." They smiled.

To Nathan, with a wink. "Good to see you."

"Yeah, likewise," Nathan managed, extending his hand.

They shook and Beal abruptly recoiled at Nathan's touch, jerking back and wincing in pain, examining his hand as though it had just been bitten by a rabid dog. The color drained from his face and he struggled to regain his composure.

"That's quite an iron grip you have," Beal said, trying to remain the diplomat, the color slowly beginning to return to his features. He couldn't resist giving Nathan a dirty look, but only for a second. It was enough. Nathan saw in the depths of those eyes that this man was capable of unfathomable evil.

When Beal's composure had returned, he told Nathan to come to his office later to discuss a business proposal. He told the guests to make themselves at home, and excused himself, saying he needed to step outside on the terrace to get some fresh air.

Beal's reaction to the white circle was not missed on the group. But Dave disappeared anyway, saying he wanted to see

Tamara. Nathan tried to encourage him to stay with the others but he knew only too well it would be like asking a cat not to chase a mouse. It was in his genes to be a womanizer and that was all there was to it.

"Be careful," Nathan said.

Stephen and Michelle were shocked at Beal's reaction to the handshake, but soon forgot about it. "Let's dance, Stephen. We're here now," she said.

"Don't worry, sweetie, we're not going far," she said to Nathan.

Nathan walked to the bar and ordered a double Scotch. He wanted to numb his rattled nerves. He walked over to one of the luxurious couches, plopped himself down and people watched. It wasn't long before a voluptuous brunette sat beside him. Cassandra eyed him seductively. Nathan recognized her. "How are you doing, sweetie?" she asked.

She wore a long, flowing black dress, plunging neckline, exposing plenty of cleavage. *Her breasts are perfect,* Nathan thought, having a hard time taking his eyes off them.

"Cheers," he said, and they clinked glasses.

"You remember me?" she asked.

"Yeah, Cassandra, we met in Santo's. And somewhere else."

"Not that I can remember," she said, inching closer to him. He had to admit, she was drop-dead gorgeous.

She put her hand on his leg, rubbing it teasingly.

There was a brief pause as Nathan enjoyed her caress.

"Beal wants to talk to you," she finally said. "He's upstairs in his office waiting. I'll see you later." She got up, smiled and winked, and walked away.

Nathan maneuvered his way upstairs, past the conversations and laughter. He reached the tall oak door at the end of the hall and knocked three times.

"Come in," Beal said.

He opened the door and entered a large dimly lit room, wall-to-wall oak bookcases filled with old classics. Beal sat at a large desk in the corner. He waved to a chair.

A fire crackled and popped in the fireplace. An expansive balcony exposed a view of downtown Vancouver in the background and an ocean view in the foreground. Beal had a drink in one hand, a Cohiba cigar in the other. Plumes of smoke formed a gray cloud above him.

The room was sticky hot. Beal had regained his composure and was fresh and alert. Nathan, on the other hand, felt his palms going clammy. He had grabbed another double Scotch on the way up the stairs and now he took a sip. He was nervous and scared but he felt the comfortably numbing effects of the alcohol settling over him. Beal offered him a cigar.

"No thanks," Nathan said, and produced one of his own cigarettes, lit it, took a long pull.

"Let's dispose of the formalities," Beal said. "I made you an offer a while ago to join me. Our observations show you as a dysfunctional, cynical boozer."

Nathan took another drink of his Scotch, as if to reinforce the statement.

"You're a shameless capitalist pig who has a pattern of getting into one unstable relationship after another."

"And your point is?"

"My point is, you're a prime candidate for our way of life. As I said before, I offer you power, money, all the women you can handle, in exchange for only one small thing."

"You want my soul."

"That's right. This place they call heaven isn't all that's it's cracked up to be, you know. A little boring, actually. Sitting around reading scripture, maybe reunited with your spouse, friends, and family. What I offer is a lascivious life of wine, women and song, all the success and money you can get your greedy little hands on. Our religious worship, like that of the Greek god Dionysus, involves orgiastic pleasures the likes of which you've never experienced."

Nathan had to admit it didn't sound bad. *Get a grip.*

"I'd like to know what happened to Andy and Mike. They're both dead, committed suicide. They both had contact with you. What did you do to them? And why?"

"They were both victims of guilty conscience. In the plural, if you like. They had the same offer you have. They both turned it down, and inevitably became haunted by their own demons. They went crazy because they were weak and vulnerable like you are."

"Are you telling me you didn't kill them?"

Nathan suspected they were haunted by demons. But not their own. He wondered what would happen to him if he turned down Beal's offer. If he would meet the same fate as Andy and Mike. He only had his experience with the Orgonions and the power of the white circle to fall back on. If it wasn't for that experience, he'd be on a different path. He knew on a gut level the key to unlocking Beal's power was with the Orgonions.

"Let's just say they had an opportunity for a better life and they didn't take it," Beal said, without admitting any culpability.

He didn't have to, as far as Nathan was concerned. Nathan just knew.

"And don't think the Orgonions have a hope in hell of stopping my progress," Beal said.

"We've known about them a long time, and believe you me their little utopia is on very shaky ground. It won't be long before they're wiped out completely."

"And how are you proposing to do that?"

"Well, let's just say they are on a path of self-destruction. And you would do well, if you want to stay among the living, to steer clear of their influence. I don't know what you're thinking, but their notions of caring and love fly directly in the face of the fundamental nature of mankind. We are by nature evil beings, prone to vice, avarice, infidelity, murder. All I do is give people what they want. I cater to their very nature. I ask you, is that such a bad thing?"

The Scotch was beginning to dull Nathan's mental faculties. "And if I don't accept your offer?"

Beal's eyes narrowed and glowed red; or was it the reflection from the flickering fire? "Your friends will die. And so will you."

Nathan stood up. He had heard enough.

"I give you fair warning now, Beal. This message comes directly from Orb. Your days are numbered. There will be a new wave of positive consciousness that will sweep the world soon, one that will cap and severely diminish your powers of influence. Heed this warning and abandon your twisted goals. I'm leaving." He offered his hand.

Beal recoiled, glaring at him. Nathan thought he noticed for the first time another look in Beal's sinister eyes; one of grave concern.

A chink in the armor, he thought, as he walked toward the door. As he closed it behind him, Beal said, "You have until midnight tonight to make up your mind. You don't want to see the result if you make the wrong decision."

Nathan joined the party of revelers. As he walked out to the pool, he noticed Stephen and Michelle, caught in an embrace, dancing to Meat Loaf's *Bat out of Hell.*

He went poolside and found Dave swimming naked in the pool with a topless Tamara.

Nathan waved Dave to the edge of the pool. "Grab a babe and hop in," Dave said.

"I think I've had enough," Nathan said, although he had to admit he was awfully tempted by many of the partially clad goddesses. "I think I'm going home, and you would be wise to join me. Please come with me."

"Are you kidding? It's early, and besides I promised Tamara we would hit the grotto later."

Nathan tried a few more times to convince Dave to leave but it was useless. *Like trying to pull a kid out of a candy store.*

"Suit yourself," he finally said, walking back into the house. "But be careful."

He convinced Michelle and Stephen to leave with him. They climbed in his van and Michelle drove them home. Nathan went straight to bed, a feeling of impending doom settling over him as he drifted off to sleep.

Chapter Twenty-Three

It was about three in the morning and Dave, very drunk and stoned by now, was back in the pool with Tamara, after spending a few pleasurable hours with her in the grotto. They had the pool to themselves. The few partiers that remained were either in the grotto or somewhere in Beal's massive house.

He frolicked with Tamara in the pool. Dave couldn't wait to get her in the grotto again. He had popped a Cialis pill after the first round, anticipating round two. He was addicted to sex and liked having it with as many women and as often as possible. Monogamy was a word that was not part of his vocabulary. He was getting a stirring in his loins just thinking about round two.

They played in the pool, jokingly dunking each other under water.

It wasn't long before the playfulness turned violent.

Tamara suddenly held his head under water. He struggled but didn't have the strength to push her away and come up for air.

She held him under, gripping him firmly by the neck. He was at least two feet below the surface and she smiled as her fingernails dug into his neck. Rivulets of blood seeped from the small wounds, snaking to the surface of the water.

His lungs ached as he tried to hold his breath. He panicked, opening his mouth to scream, inhaling mouthfuls of water. He felt his strength draining, lungs filling with water. *Fuck, she's drowning me. What a way to go.*

In a last ditch effort, he flipped backwards, out of her grip momentarily, and landed a hard kick, flush on her jaw.

Dazed, she fell backwards—a flash knock out. She stood up shaking her head, trying to clear the cobwebs. She slowly walked toward him, a sinister look in her eyes.

He surfaced, hacking and coughing, trying to breathe. He vomited up a milky liquid, coughed again, and drew a breath.

But Tamara was on him again and she was angry. She was within inches of grabbing his throat and Dave inhaled a big gulp of air, dove underwater. He thanked his mother for insisting he go to swimming lessons when he was just a boy.

Tamara dove down after him, grabbing onto his ankle. He squirmed and struggled as he towed her around the pool, trying to shake her grip. It felt like he was in the metal teeth of a bear trap. Tamara wouldn't let go.

Dave was getting weaker by the second and he wondered what it would be like to die. Given the way he had lived his life, his disregard for the emotions of women and a reckless pursuit of material gain, he doubted very much he would end up in heaven—if such a place even existed.

If I can only make it to the edge of the pool. Just need something to grab onto, give me some leverage to get out of this damned bear trap. Then he was at the edge.

He was just about to grab onto the metal staircase leading from the pool, when he felt himself being dragged underwater, about three feet or so.

This is it. This is what's it's like to die. Realizing he was in the shallow end, he put one foot down, raised the other foot that Tamara held, and in one motion, as he saw her head surface with the ankle she clutched, he swung around, throwing all his weight into a spinning back fist. He connected with a large cracking sound. Tamara released her grip, squealed and fell backwards into the pool with a loud splash.

Dave also fell back with the momentum of the blow. The adrenaline kicking in, he stood, ran to the edge of the pool, leaping up on the patio. He glanced back momentarily at Tamara, noticing blood trickling from a nose that was definitely out of joint. Broken. She put her head down, hand to her face, catching some of the dripping blood.

"Come back," she shouted as Dave, buck-naked, ran into some thick bushes. "I was just playing. I got carried away."

He didn't look back. He ran across the lawn, down the driveway toward the large entrance gates. They were locked. He climbed the fence swiftly. Heard the sound of barking dogs coming closer, closer, then snapping at his heals, leaping up the fence, narrowly missing him. He glanced down as he climbed. Two pit bulls barked and snarled ferociously.

He reached the top of the gates, speared his leg on one of the protruding spikes. It had penetrated at least three inches and he winced in pain. He jerked his leg free in one motion. It squirted blood. "Fuck." He jumped from the eight-foot high gate, spraining his ankle as he landed.

"Shit, fucking son of a bitch," he said as he winced in pain, limping down the dark and winding road.

His twisted ankle was screaming out in pain and he was losing a lot of blood from his leg wound. He limped along shivering. He saw headlights in the distance and started waving his hands, trying to flag the vehicle over.

It whizzed past.

He was in a state. Wiping his wound, he had smeared blood all over his leg, on his chest, all over his face. "Who is going to pull over?" he asked, as he limped along, a full moon illuminating his path. A dog barked as if in response to his rhetorical question.

He saw more headlights coming toward him in the blackness. He flailed his hands. What choice did he have? The car slowed. It looked like a woman. The car was black, a sports car, but Dave could not make out the model. It was the last thing on his mind.

A blonde woman eyed him as she slowly passed, horrified. She sped away, squealing the tires and spitting gravel at him. One rock careened off his head, gouged it, and he felt a trickle of blood roll into his eye.

"Fucking bitch," he said, flipping the bird.

He continued down the gravel road toward the main highway. He passed large estate homes and thought about knocking on the door of one. *They probably have dogs also. And even if someone did answer the door were they really likely to open it?* As well, the formidable wrought iron gates made the home look like a fortress. He shivered and walked on.

More lights approached in the distance. As the lights became brighter, the vehicle's speed increased, much too fast for the windy road. It approached him and abruptly skidded to a stop. Dave jumped into the ditch to avoid a shower of flying rocks.

"Dave, Dave, is that you?" Nathan asked. He had bolted upright at three in the morning and felt certain that Dave was in grave danger. He had dressed in a hurry, and drove by Dave's apartment. After buzzing countless times, even pitching rocks at the window, he had driven out to Beal's house, in the hope of rescuing his friend. When he saw the figure staggering on the road, he knew it had to be Dave. That's when he had floored it.

"Get me out of here," Dave said, his voice verging on panic.

After driving Dave to his apartment, helping him into some clothes, and wrapping a clean t-shirt around the leg wound, Nathan drove to the hospital. Dave had filled Nathan in on what happened and the realization was beginning to sink in. He had come very close to dying.

"You okay?" Nathan asked, searching Dave's face for some kind of expression.

"I'll be okay," Dave said, not so reassuringly. "Just need some time to deal with this. Should have listened to you."

Nathan sat in the waiting room while the doctors attended to Dave. He waited four hours, and watched patients, nurses, doctors, coming and going. At one point a man was wheeled in on a stretcher, flailing his arms, blood still streaming from bandages on his wrists.

Staff wrestled to contain him, finally popped him in a wheelchair and took him away. As the man passed Nathan, his eyes widened in horror: "I've seen the devil ... and he's coming to get you."

Nathan thought he recognized the man from Beal's party but couldn't be sure. He shuddered and waited.

A little while later, he drove Dave home. He had his leg stitched, a tensor bandage on the ankle and three stitches in his forehead, the handiwork of the woman with the squealing tires. He pulled in front of Dave's apartment.

"Next time I'll listen to you," Dave said as he stepped out of the car. It was daylight and Nathan could already feel the vehicle's interior warming with the sun's rays.

"There may not be a next time," Nathan said. "You listen to me now. Stay the fuck away from Beal, Tamara, that entire corridor of the city."

Chapter Twenty-Four

Three days later, Nathan snaked his way through rush hour traffic, on his way home after running some errands. He wondered if and when he would return to Orgon. He was ready, especially with Beal fucking up everyone he came into contact with.

He went through a mental checklist. He had met with Michelle earlier in the week and signed over power of attorney to her, as well as made arrangements for her to adopt his beloved cat, Matty. She would also deal with his apartment and the deal on Sal's. His BC acreage, well, he owned it clear title. It could just sit there.

He had also warned Michelle, Stephen and Dave again to stay away from Beal. Beal had given him until midnight to join his camp. And he hadn't. His warning to Beal hardly seemed sufficient but what else was he to say? He had no idea of how to neutralize Beal. He was very tired and sleep overcame him quickly for a change.

He soared above the Earth in a spaceship, noticing how mankind had ravaged it, clearing large tracts for urban development, industry and agriculture. It became a tiny dot in a vast universe of many little dots.

He opened his eyes. Ophelia, her smooth white skin glowing, was beside him, still sleeping. Nathan thought he was dreaming. He closed his eyes momentarily, opened them again. Ophelia was still there. He looked around the room, taking in its minimalist beauty. A bay window overlooked a well-manicured lawn, with lush green hedges bordering it.

Beyond, a majestic forest, trees looming large and ominous and the soothing sound of a babbling brook. He surveyed the room. A control panel was on the wall just above his head and slightly to the left of the gigantic oval-shaped bed. End tables bracketed either side of the bed, each with touch-control, futuristically sleek lamps.

There was a simple vanity near the bay window, a small mirror and an ergonomically correct chair. He imagined that's where Ophelia made herself beautiful but he couldn't identify the accoutrements on the table. A large burgundy couch was to the left of the bay window, a simple but comfortable armchair beside it and a small black coffee table. On it was a model of the solar system, but the configuration of planets didn't much resemble Earth's solar system. The walls were a deep greenish-brown, finished with modern black trim, giving the room a tranquil, soothing feeling.

"You're awake," Ophelia said, leaning over and gently kissing his cheek. It gave him goose bumps. She turned him on big-time. "I've been waiting for you," she said, rolling over and exposing a partial view of a perky breast. He leaned over, enveloping Ophelia in a warm embrace, kissing her passionately. Then he remembered the problems on Earth and the mood left him.

"Ophelia, wait."

She stopped caressing him, rolled over on her belly, propped her chin into her hands and said playfully, "What's the matter?" But she saw his furrowed brow and knew it was serious.

"It's your friends," she said. "They are not out of danger yet, are they?"

"No, they're not. And before I left here last time I should've at least figured out how to get rid of Beal. I guess I haven't been thinking too clearly. How can I stay here knowing my friends are in eminent danger?"

"Calm down, my dear," Ophelia said soothingly. "You remember Orb said you can't really get rid of Beal types. They will just be replaced by another, unless the susceptible ones somehow reprogram their minds. That's part of the reason you're here. To learn our ways, teach Earthlings a new way of thinking."

"Fair enough," Nathan said. "But Orb said I would be able to neutralize Beal. I didn't. He threatened the lives of three of my friends if I don't join his camp. I managed to give him fair warning that his days are numbered and he seemed to take the threat seriously enough. But, of course, I didn't sell my soul. I was supposed to give him an answer a few days ago and I didn't. And my friend Dave was almost killed by Tamara."

"Okay, okay, we will talk to my father again about this. See what he suggests this time. But couldn't we do something else first?" Ophelia rolled back on top of Nathan and this time the blanket slipped away, exposing two very perky and full breasts. She kissed him softly.

Nathan was about to protest but his member had a different game plan. He thought about what Ophelia had said. It sounded reasonable. Talk to Orb again.

Nathan started returning her kisses and they made love. He enjoyed wave after wave of intense pleasure and finally shuddered with a powerful orgasm. Ophelia arched her back, moaning with enjoyment, tightened her grip, let out a final satisfied moan as she came. They both relaxed, Nathan collapsing on top of Ophelia, breathing deeply.

She pressed a button on the control panel and Maiden whirred into the room, large tray in its metal hands with food and drink. Maiden expertly wheeled the tray to the foot of the bed, adjusted a metal table underneath it, and slid it toward the satisfied lovers.

"Breakfast Ophelia," Maiden said, acknowledging Nathan with a cheery smile.

The robot circled and zipped out of the room.

I could get used to this, Nathan thought, as he sipped a hot black liquid that tasted something like coffee.

About an hour later they were in the living room addressing Orb. "Maybe I wasn't crystal-clear last time we spoke," Nathan said to the screen. "I thought you would give me some power to deal with Beal. Well, he definitely got jolted by the white circle, whatever power that seems to have, but it didn't take him out."

Nathan glanced again at his palm, noticing the white circle had all but disappeared. He had gone over the events at Beal's party with Orb but Orb only nodded as if he already knew these things.

"You mentioned you cannot get rid of a Beal type but this didn't really sink in since you were also giving me some special power to deal with him. I'm worried about my friends. Do you have a solution?"

The screen stayed silent for a few moments. Finally Orb spoke. "Orgonions cannot promote the use of violence to ward off a threat. As a race, we can only use violence in the defense of our lives and the preservation of our planet."

"I think this qualifies," Nathan said. "I think he has you in his sights."

"No, it doesn't," Orb responded. "But I may have a solution to the problem. That white circle you were given represents a special power that we on Orgon have managed to harness and use to our advantage in deadly situations. We gave it to you to help you with your negotiations, and also help you ward off the threat of Beal. If you notice, you don't have it anymore. It's not needed on Orgon."

"I still don't see where you're going with this."

"If you are saying that you need an assurance that they are out of danger before you commit to Orgon, we can give you that."

"How?"

"Simple little white circles inserted on the hands of your friends. Programmed specifically to last for four months, giving us a chance to think through a more permanent solution. The circles will repel any and all attacks from Beal or his recruitment forces."

Nathan didn't have a clue how the power worked and probably never would. But it seemed like a good temporary solution at least until better minds than his could solve the problem. Or, begin reprogramming the minds of Earth's inhabitants so they would be less susceptible to Beal's evil influence.

"How do we get these circles onto the palms of my friends?" he asked. "Do they have to come up here?"

"No. Ophelia will show you how. We can imprint each one from Orgon. Are we finished here and do we have an agreement?"

Nathan had no reason to doubt Orb. He marveled at the speed with which Orb had managed to temporarily solve a problem that had Nathan stupefied. "Uh ... am I allowed any communication with my friends while I'm here?"

"If we are to reform you and you are to become a student of our way of life, we don't want that. We will, however, take you up to our dream control room where Ophelia will help you imprint the white circles on their palms. Is that it then?" Orb seemed interested in returning to his governing duties, whatever they might consist of.

Nathan nodded and the screen faded to black.

Chapter Twenty-Five

They were in the control room situated in one of the mushroom-shaped buildings at the top of a hill the glider had whisked them to with incredible speed. Nathan sat in a gray steel chair with a soft leathery cushion.

He marveled at the walls of computer screens, rows and rows of what appeared to be hard drives, some of them illuminated with flickering lights. Other computer screens displayed a myriad of different images resembling either a galaxy, solar system or constellation, Nathan could not be sure.

On still another screen, brightly colored geometric shapes danced in and out of focus. The display baffled Nathan and he wasn't eager to learn the intricacies and reasons for all this technology. There would be enough time for that later.

He wanted to be sure that his friends were safe, even if only temporarily. He felt Orb would eventually discover a permanent solution. *Or was that even possible?*

Ophelia snapped him out of his thoughts. "You seem so preoccupied. Please try and relax." Nathan looked at her and wondered how a woman who looked so plain on one hand could also be so beautiful.

He remembered his recent relationship woes and it seemed to him the way he handled the situation with Lena and Adelita was immature. That thought had never dawned on him before, with his self-righteous, selfish and arrogant attitude.

Some things were coming clear.

"Hey, wake up," Ophelia said, approaching with a large black headset. "Try and stay with me in the now, at least while I explain our technology to you."

"Isn't that a little invasive to their privacy? I mean, entering their private dreams?"

"Don't worry about anything like that," Ophelia declared matter-of-factly. "You will enter their dreams for only a flash, deposit the circle and a subconscious message will be recorded by your friends telling them how long the circle will last. They will wake up refreshed and secure in the knowledge that they have some temporary protection from Beal."

Ophelia explained the device. She told him after it was strapped into place, and he was buckled in the reclining chair, she would adjust the controls and Nathan would slip into a dream travel state. The device would guide him through the process.

Nathan fastened his seatbelt and Ophelia adjusted the controls.

The lights in his head grew dim.

Chapter Twenty-Six

Dave Healy dreamt he was making love to Tamara, drenched in sweat, missionary position. He pounded into her furiously and it felt good. Real good. He reached the verge of orgasm and looked into her eyes. They had turned a fiery red and her face contorted into the image of a snake. She hissed and her features darkened. Dave tried to escape. He couldn't move. Raw panic enveloped him. Tamara gripped into his back with her fingernails piercing the skin. Rivulets of blood dripped down his back but he was helpless to stop her attack.

He tried to scream but his lips wouldn't move. Tamara clutched him tighter and said two words: "You die!"

For fuck sakes, this must really be it this time. The haunting memory of his last encounter was still fresh in his mind.

Then a sudden blinding flash of white light, and he woke up in bed. Tamara had disappeared. Slowly the digital red letters on his alarm clock came into focus: 6:67 am.

He was horrified. But the feelings of dread were mixed with a tingling feeling of positive energy. He tried to get up but his back hurt. He let his eyes adjust to the light of the blue moon seeping through the Venetian blinds and focused on the bed sheets. They were soaked with sweat. And something else. Blood. He touched his back and could feel the cuts, and they ached, along with his still throbbing sprained ankle and puncture wound.

"What the fuck just happened?" He lifted his hand to wipe the sweat from his brow and then he noticed it. A white glowing circle, and with the recognition of that image came the immediate realization that Nathan was somehow responsible for it; and the circle had somehow saved his life. He rubbed it. It felt warm to the touch. He felt protected.

Michelle sat at her kitchen table sipping a coffee and sucking on a cigarette. Stephen moved about the kitchen economically, preparing breakfast; eggs benedict. A good cook, he prepared a lot of the meals. They had a deal. When Stephen cooked, Michelle would clean, and it worked well.

Michelle felt weird. She remembered having a nightmare last night. She was running through an old-growth forest, being chased by someone whom she believed to be Beal. "Come," he kept calling after her. "I won't hurt you." But she knew it wasn't true.

She believed if she stopped for a second, Beal would overtake and kill her. She ran through the brush, panting and panting, becoming short of breath.

Her progress was slow and she heard him gaining. Suddenly she reached the end of the road. She saw a cliff and nowhere else to go. She stopped, literally skidded right to the edge and looked down. It was a black hole, infinite in depth. If she fell, she might fall forever.

Beal was right behind her now, regarding her threateningly. "Looks like you've run out of real estate," he had said sarcastically, all the while inching forward, arms outstretched.

Michelle remembered trying to move, but couldn't. She was frozen. She fixed her gaze on Beal and tried to speak but no words came. Then it happened. He rushed forward and pushed her hard off the edge of the cliff. This time she did scream, a loud shriek that formed two words: "Heeeeellllllllllllp meeeeeeeeeeeee!!!"

She remembered falling swiftly while her life passed before her in a flash. Some of it she regretted, like her selfish attitude. She could have been a little more caring and compassionate. Her choices when it came to men, always seeming to pick the bad boys, present company not necessarily excluded. Her reckless pursuit of material gain and the mistaken belief that accomplishing material goals equaled happiness.

Then it happened. A bolt of white light penetrated her entire being, filling her with joy and she woke up, her sheer nightgown soaked in sweat. She opened her eyes, bewildered, looking for the familiar company of Stephen. But he was not in bed. She had sat quiet for a moment and listened. She could hear the familiar rustling sounds of Stephen making coffee in the kitchen. She touched the sleeve of her nightgown, feeling how wet it was with perspiration and noticed the circle on her right palm. She looked at it intently. It glowed and felt warm to the touch. She thought of Nathan and knew she was safe.

"I can't believe something like this can actually happen," she said, while Stephen sat down next to her, placing an appetizing plate of steaming eggs benedict on the table. Funny thing though. Although Stephen had said nothing to this point, she had noticed the same circle on his right palm and he appeared more chipper than usual.

"I'm sure you noticed this," he said finally between mouthfuls of food, exposing his right palm to Michelle.

"Yes, I did," she said, between bites. "I meant to ask you about your experience but was so preoccupied and ... I don't know, changed, from my experience."

"I had a nightmare last night," Stephen said. He explained to Michelle that his nightmare was almost entirely sexual in nature. He was in a dimly lit chamber of sorts, making love to two beautiful women. One of them was going down on him and the other was squatting on his face. During the sex, babel echoed distantly from adjoining corridors.

The building itself seemed to be made up of a series of interlocking corridors, with different chambers situated along the way, with no distinct pattern. He remembered being on the verge of an intense orgasm when one woman's head had transformed into a reticulated python. Then her legs became the body of the python and wrapped around his neck, choking off his breath and causing him to gasp for air in panic. At the moment he felt he was going to black out, the white thunderbolt of light had penetrated his body and he lay drenched in sweat on his bed, Michelle still sleeping not so soundly beside him.

"Something else," he said, finishing the story. "Check this out," he said, exposing his neck and some rather nasty looking red welts. "This scares the shit out of me." Stephen was not one to mince words. But he was acting quite differently this morning, less arrogant and sarcastic than usual.

Chapter Twenty-Seven

Nathan sat in a comfortable chair atop a mammoth backhoe, and worked the computerized controls. He scooped up a huge load of gravelly material and expertly swung the bucket toward the waiting dump truck. Weelie, a small white man with large curious green eyes, matching coveralls and hardhat, sat in the waiting dump truck watching him, a wry grin on his face. He was always joking around. "You're taking forever, Natan," Weelie said. That's just how he pronounced it. "My grandmother can go faster than you and she's 140 years old."

She probably was 140 years old, Nathan thought; as Ophelia had once told him Orgonions could live for 200 years and it was rumored Orb was over 200.

"Shut your pie hole, you little twerp," Nathan responded. "Your truck is full so get the hell outta here." Nathan winced a little at the word hell as it still brought back vague memories of his experiences with Beal.

Weelie smiled a toothy grin, revved the motor on the monster truck, and drove down the road toward the refining facility, where he would deposit the load for the Orgonions to sift through and extract the uranium to power planet Orgon, before returning for another load.

Usually another dump truck would be right behind Weelie, but one of the trucks had broken down earlier so he had a few minutes to wait before Weelie would return.

He adjusted some of the computerized controls on the huge backhoe, put the scoop down level on the ground stabilizing the large piece of equipment, flipped open the cabin door, pulled out a skinny white smoke, lit it and inhaled deeply, enjoying the view of the mountains and the sunset.

He had worked nine hours at the uranium mine, helping to do whatever he could for the Orgonions. He drew on his smoke and reflected on his month on Orgon. He found the Orgonions pretty reasonable people. It was refreshing that they were not caught up in the rat-race like humans, wildly pursuing material wealth only to discover when they retired they were usually too old and frail to enjoy the fruits of their labor.

And unlike many Earth inhabitants, they tried to live in harmony with nature.

Nathan didn't like the materialistic thinking that was ingrained in human consciousness. The entire industrialized world was geared to producing, consuming, dumping, and destroying the planet. And while humans had the technology to live in harmony with nature, for the most part the desire was not yet there. It would take a major shift in the way humans think and he wondered if he would ever live to see a world where people's thoughts and actions weren't driven by the need for consumer goods.

Humans needed to slow down and smell the roses, he thought. During his classes at Orgon University, he discovered foremost among the Orgonion tenants of living was an appreciation and respect for nature.

Three times a week, he would hop on an air glider, fly five minutes along the super air highway, and arrive at a metal and glass building where he studied The Orgon Doctrine. He liked the planet so much that Earth had become almost a distant memory. His life had become pleasantly domesticated, and he didn't have the same caustic edge he once had.

He could still feel it just below the surface at times, but also felt the seeds of change beginning to take root.

His attraction to Ophelia had deepened by the day. She was dynamite in bed, loyal and caring.

She also had an uncanny ability to predict what was on his mind. It was impossible to lie to her. As well, he made a promise to himself that he wouldn't lie to her. So far it had worked.

So he helped in the garden, worked the mines, went to school, and once a week he would update Orb on his progress. He was happy here and at times wondered if he even wanted to return to Earth.

But the cause was one of the noblest mankind could ever undertake; a mission to save the human race and save the planet from self-destruction.

He often wondered if he was the right man for the job, if he really had the intestinal fortitude to pull it off.

A large black spaceship caught his eye and snapped him out of his introspection. He noticed the spaceship was not circling in the same direction as it had previously. He knew Urellians guarded the Orgonion skies with large spaceships, designed to ward off invasive forces.

But their presence had increased. Nathan puzzled at this, but a whistling noise made him forget the thought.

Weelie had returned for another load of gravel. He often whistled to get Nathan's attention, and it didn't bother Nathan in the least. He liked Weelie and the two had become good friends and often joked around. "Hey, Natan, get the mammoth monster going and fill me up."

"You got it, Pontiac," Nathan said, fired up his backhoe, and in three quick button-press motions, had the large scoop whirring toward a pile of gravel. He scooped it up and in the next instant it was deposited into Weelie's waiting dump truck.

Weelie didn't understand the reference and regarded him curiously.

Thirty-five minutes later they sat in the refinery cafeteria, drinking coffee. Perked you up just fine but contained no caffeine. The other workers were mostly gone, or heading out on their air gliders.

Nathan and Weelie chatted. This was their ritual before parting company. They joked around for the first few minutes, but the increased presence of the Urellian spaceships and the deviant flying pattern disturbed Nathan and he changed the subject. "I notice a lot more Urellian spaceships. It's giving me a bad feeling. Are they preparing to attack?"

"Not to my knowledge," Weelie said. "I do know that we have a conference coming up soon to resign our peace pact with the Urellians but I doubt there is a problem. And, I didn't notice the ships more often than usual."

Nathan wasn't comfortable with the explanation but decided to let it go for now. He wanted to return home to Ophelia. "Let's forget it for now, my friend. Until tomorrow."

Weelie waved goodbye.

As Nathan left, he saw three Urellian ships flying overhead, the most he had ever seen so close together. Two disappeared and the other one hovered above him.

Something's wrong. He could feel it.

Nathan never tired of the experience he had on the air glider. He whirred along the air highway, his speed reaching 180 kilometers an hour on a few straight stretches. A few air gliders passed him, but not many.

Nathan was addicted to speed and he cracked the side window slightly so he could feel the wind whipping past.

He looked forward to a night with Ophelia, in his new domestic existence on this faraway planet.

Twenty minutes later, he was sitting at the dinner table finishing his meal; barbequed salmon, mashed potatoes, corn, bean sprouts and a small fruit salad for dessert. Nathan had for the last month educated Ophelia on some of the ways Earthlings prepared food. She had gone to great pains to learn the recipes to please her man. She had also taught Maiden a few Earth recipes.

Nathan shoveled the last of his meal, mashed potatoes and corn, into his mouth, chewed it slowly, savoring the flavor, and eyed Ophelia. She looked especially radiant tonight and had gone to great effort to create a romantic mood. She had even adjusted the lighting.

On the kitchen table was a replica of an oil lantern, electrically powered. In the living room, the bay window let in the soft glow of moonlight. On the two end tables, on either side of the plush living room couch, two more replica oil lanterns glowed. With the moonlight seeping into the room, stars glimmering in the distance, and the yellow light of the oil lanterns radiating onto the deep green walls, the image looked almost surreal. Some jazz music played in the background. Nathan was enjoying himself.

She winked at him with one of her big green eyes, eyes that for Nathan had now become so compelling. "You seem off in a trance today, honey, but I'm so glad to see the corners of your lips now pointing up, instead of down. You seem at peace here."

"I am very happy here, dear," Nathan said, smiling. "I'm learning a lot about your culture and customs and feel hungry for more knowledge." Nathan couldn't resist getting up briefly to plant a long wet kiss on Ophelia's lips. He returned to his seat and said, "You make me very happy."

"I hope so," Ophelia said. "That is my highest priority."

Nathan thought about mentioning the increased ship presence to Ophelia but tomorrow was another day. He had refinery work in the morning, a four-hour break in the afternoon during which he would squeeze in a meeting with Orb and then Orgon University.

Perhaps I'll mention it to Orb tomorrow? Why ruin this magical moment? This woman makes me crazy. He stood up, walked over to Ophelia, gently took her by the hand and led her out into the garden. They sat on a plush bench and contemplated life. As they left, Maiden whirred into the room with a greeting and started cleaning up.

Nathan could talk to Ophelia for hours and she was such an eager listener. Although she had received an education about Earth, it obviously was not the same as being there. And, she had been told many things about Nathan, but not everything. Nathan enjoyed learning about the Orgonion culture and he wanted to know more about Ophelia; but he also felt he wanted to get some things off his chest. It felt good to tell Ophelia of his troubled childhood, and some of the unfortunate circumstances of his past.

By telling her, he felt like it was a cleansing of sorts, as though he was liberating himself from the bad memories so they would no longer be a part of who he was. And Ophelia had a sharp, inquisitive mind. She really wanted to learn about the complexities of Nathan to better understand him and by extension be better equipped to please him.

He told her about his alcoholic, abusive father, about his very caring mother, about his two sisters and one brother and how they grew up on the mean streets of Brantford on very little. Compared to worldwide standards of poverty, Nathan supposed they lived rather well, as they were always able to eat. But at some meals, not all food groups were represented.

And, since Nathan had received little parental guidance growing up, he had joined a street gang at the tender age of fourteen and got into all kinds of trouble. Of course, this juvenile record was now wiped clean, and Nathan had quit school and left Brantford before he could get into serious trouble.

He learned a few years after he left that most of his friends had landed in jail, one of them even for murder. As the story went, there were three of them strung out on heroin. They ran out of the drug, came down hard and needed money to buy more. Nathan's friend Mitchell accompanied two other guys (unknown to Nathan) into an underground parking lot, robbed a woman of her purse and its contents and one of them pulled a gun, shot and killed her. Although Mitchell had not pulled the trigger, the prosecutor was able to show intent to kill and therefore Mitchell was convicted of second-degree murder and served 10 years in prison.

He also told her of the time he was first initiated into the gang and had to prove his worthiness to the other gang members. The initiation they put him through involved picking a fight with a new kid on the block. Although Geritt had done nothing to aggravate or anger the gang, it was Nathan's job to show him The Diving Devils owned the streets.

The memory of that fight had stayed with Nathan and bothered him. He supposed he would have felt better if Geritt had fought back. But he didn't. He just took Nathan's repeated punches and kicks, curled up in a ball on the sidewalk. When he eventually got up, bruised and battered, he ran home to his mother, crying.

The Devils were feared in the neighborhood so there were no repercussions. None of the neighbors, or even Geritt's mother, would do anything.

The Devils believed they could get away with murder.

Ophelia caressed Nathan's face gently, searching his eyes. Now, she had a look of sadness in those beautiful eyes and Nathan was suddenly sorry he had told her so much so soon. He felt like he had ruined an otherwise perfect night.

"I'm sorry, baby," he said. "It feels so good to finally tell someone. I've never told anyone this before and I suppose I wanted to get it off my chest. You are just such a great listener."

"No problem," Ophelia said. "But perhaps it's enough for one night. I don't want to see you become too upset. And I can see the sadness in your eyes when you talk of these things."

"You're right. It's behind. Not important." He caressed her face gently and kissed her. "Let's go to bed, before I fall asleep in your lap. Thank you for listening. And thank you for being you. I'm crazy about you."

Chapter Twenty-Eight

The next day Nathan sat next to Weelie in a large white lecture hall. At the podium, barely visible, was a thin white man with a long white beard and big green eyes. He was dressed in a black one-piece suit that looked like it had been painted on.

Above him was a large screen and when he needed to emphasize a particular point about The Orgon Doctrine he would rely on his high-tech visual aids. The lecture hall was not much different to the ones Nathan had attended in university. It was shaped like a theatre hall, acoustically designed so the sound would travel up to the highest row of chairs to the very back, where Nathan sat.

To walk to the podium also meant a descent of about fifty feet, down a number of stairs. That's why Professor Wilks looked so small. He was very far away. But his voice could be heard crystal-clear and Nathan scrawled copious notes on his computer tablet, as did the hundred or so other Orgonions, all of whom looked much younger than Nathan.

He listened as Wilks talked. There were eighteen commandments to the Orgonion Doctrine and Wilks tended to jump around quite a bit and did not discuss them in chronological order.

"Do not commit adultery, unless liaisons with other partners is specifically outlined in your contract," Wilks said. Nathan found this one rather interesting. With so many marriages breaking down on Earth due to infidelity, and the divorce rate rising rapidly, the Orgonions had found a way around this. You simply signed a contract that would either permit or disallow extramarital affairs.

They also had the seven-year-itch problem solved. It was well documented on Earth that couples, legally married or common law unions, tended to get bored with the relationship after seven years. Nathan's marriage had lasted almost seven years to the day before they realized their lives were going in different directions and divorced.

Other than some obvious disagreements and goals, normal for any long-term union, the break-up seemed to come down to one simple thing—she wanted kids and he didn't.

Wilks continued. "If you do sign a contract that permits a liaison with one other partner, for example, choose a partner who has a similar contract or at least knows of your other contractual obligations and will accept a relationship within those boundaries. Never, ever solicit a man's wife who has signed a mutually exclusive contract or you will end up on Pluton."

Pluton, Nathan learned, was where the criminals went. Since Pluton was aligned with Orgon, they had agreed to build a facility to house the deviants in exchange for plutonium and uranium. Nathan had heard the "reform centers" were not well populated and the reform rate was excellent.

Ophelia's cousin had landed on Pluton by breaching a marital contract. Two years later, he was back on Orgon and a very productive member of society. Reform treatment had a lot to do with positive reinforcement, with an absence of cruel measures like solitary confinement that was used in some Earth prisons.

In many cases, Earth prisoners left the prison system hardened and beyond rehabilitation, the opposite of the prison mandate. Cruel and inhumane methods of rehabilitation were not to be found on Pluton and prisoners also had the option of remaining on Pluton after they served out their prison term to make a fresh start.

"You have to take a very deep and introspective look at yourself before getting into any contract with another partner," Wilks said. "And it is mandatory here that you be at least twenty-one before signing a union contract."

The rest of Wilks's lecture consisted of outlining the various types of contracts that were available to Orgonions. They included: The seven-year mutually exclusive, the seven-year contract solely for child rearing with love not necessarily a part of it, and two, four and six year contracts which had variations of terms in the seven-year contracts.

"Okay," he finished. "We're out of time so no questions. See you next time. Read chapter six and seven in your computer tablet and do the exercises. Quiz next week. Oh, I want you to do an exercise that's not in the book. Think about the contracts we have. Tell me what you like and don't like about them. Compare them to the marriage contracts on Earth. As well, do you have a suggestion on a new relationship contract that perhaps Orgonion law does not cover yet?"

Chapter Twenty-Nine

Nathan raced down the air highway on his air glider. He had just finished a quick coffee with Weelie and he wanted to discuss some things with Orb. He learned Weelie was two years into a seven-year mutually exclusive contract with his wife, Eve. They planned on having two kids and renewing their contract with the same terms once it had expired. Weelie wasn't typical of many Earth males; he only wanted one woman.

Nathan knew a lot of men who disliked monogamy and wanted multiple partners. Weelie was nothing like that. He seemed to dote on Eve, and hardly even looked at other female Orgonions. Nathan wished he could say the same for himself.

Although he was enamored with Ophelia, he sure couldn't help his wandering eyes. He had noticed many well-endowed females on Orgon.

As he rounded a corner, Nathan saw the Urellian ships again, more of them and closer than before. He had kept this observation from Ophelia so far, not wanting to panic her, but had mentioned it again to Weelie just before departing. This time Weelie admitted the pattern and frequency of the spaceships was unusual and disturbing.

A black cop air glider suddenly appeared right beside Nathan and a message flashed on his computer screen panel. 'Watch your speed. And watch where you're going,' the message said.

The officer looked over to determine if Nathan had read and understood the message. Nathan gave him the thumbs up, flashed a white light and decreased his speed.

The officer sped away.

That was the second warning Nathan had been given by the same cop and Ophelia had told him one more and he would get a ticket which would cost the household credits, credits that Nathan had worked hard at the refinery to accumulate. He made a mental note to be more cautious and carried on down the air highway at the posted speed limit—140 kilometers an hour.

He was thinking of his meeting with Orb, as he zipped up the driveway with the air glider and expertly parked it in the garage of their twelve hundred square-foot, three-bedroom, dome-shaped white bungalow.

Chapter Thirty

After a light salad dinner, he sat on the living room couch with Ophelia and talked about The Orgon Doctrine. He was curious to examine all of its commandments and get her take on them. Before speaking, he reviewed the material.

The Orgon Doctrine

1. Consider others before you consider yourself.

2. The pursuit of material gain is a self-centered goal ultimately destined for unhappiness and dissatisfaction.

3. Cherish family and friends; these bonds should be loyal and lasting.

4. Judge yourself before you judge others.

5. Do not steal.

6. Treat others fairly, with love and respect.

7. Do not strike another person except in the preservation of your life, the life of your loved ones or the protection of your planet.

8. Do not commit adultery, unless it is specified in your contract.

9. Do not kill.

10. Accept that there are many higher powers in the universe without attaching these higher powers to any specific religious denomination.

11. All beings on all planets were created equal.

12. Do not lie.

13. Do not wrongfully desire your neighbor's wife, family, house, animals or other possessions.

14. Understand jealousy is a powerful and useless emotion. Do not harbor this emotion.

15. Treat your planet and all living organisms with the upmost respect and care at all times.

16. Be happy in the moment. The past is history and the future is unknown.

17. Learn to forgive.

18. Think positively and avoid negative thoughts. You are the only one responsible for the way you feel. Another being cannot make you feel sad. It is your perception of an event that will dictate your reaction to it. Look for the positive in all of your experiences and dealings with individuals from all planets.

Ophelia and Nathan worked on the homework assignment together. Nathan had read the two chapters, answered the questions, and was now wrestling with what Wilks had said:

How do the Orgonion marriage contracts compare to those of Earth? Is there something missing in the Orgonion contracts or something that can be improved upon?

"I like the Orgonion seven-year mutually exclusive contract much better than Earth's traditional marriage contract," Ophelia said. "With your marriage contracts, if a divorce occurs, I am told that in many cases lawyers get involved and it becomes a fight for money, usually the man's money. And he usually loses and then develops a bitter attitude about relationships and marriage in general. This contributes to a cynical attitude among both parties. With our contract, the parties can mutually agree to sever it, but we do not have the financial implications that you do therefore there is less chance that a man, or a woman, would develop such a sinister attitude about relationships. It is only when money becomes involved that this factors in."

Nathan had to admit, for someone who had never been to Earth, Ophelia certainly had a pretty good grasp about the Earthly institution of marriage. "Point taken," he said. "And a good one at that."

He was taking the role of devil's advocate. "But, what about this seven-year contract that allows each partner to have outside sexual liaisons? Couldn't this lead to jealousy and resentment and damage an otherwise good relationship? Case studies in Canada, for example, have shown that polygamy doesn't work. In many cases, the women come to resent sharing their husband with one, or sometimes several women."

Ophelia paused for a moment. "You have a point. But, think about it this way. If a man is not genetically predisposed for monogamy, wouldn't our contract allow for him to have a mistress without fear of reprisals, financial and emotional? As well, he could do it openly so he wouldn't have to live a life of lies with his spouse. I have heard of some small villages in Mexico where it is accepted by a man's wife that he have a mistress and they almost expect it of him."

Nathan remembered reading something similar. How could he counter this argument? Perhaps there was some merit to both contracts and perhaps there was no right answer; just different points of view. And Ophelia's point of view seemed to work for the Orgonions.

He suspected that Ophelia very much liked this discussion. He could see the way she became animated talking of a seven-year, mutually exclusive contract. Even though she was well aware that Nathan was being groomed to become a disciple of The Orgon Doctrine, she seemed to hold out some hope of a future with him. And she was Orb's daughter, after all.

Perhaps the Orgonions had a master plan that Nathan was yet to fully comprehend?

With that thought the lights dimmed and the big screen in front of him flashed on. Nathan had become so engrossed in conversation with Ophelia, he had almost forgotten about his meeting with Orb.

"Let's pick up this discussion another time, dear," he said, seconds before the image on the big screen came into focus.

"Hello, Nathan," Orb said, smiling at his daughter. "Let us review a few things shall we?"

Nathan responded to Orb's questions. He told him he was happy on Orgon, enjoyed his life with Ophelia, liked his work at the mine, and more or less thought The Orgon Doctrine was a fine piece of work.

Orb changed the subject. "You may have heard about an upcoming meeting we have with the other planets. Soon they will be arriving at our governing temple to discuss the terms of re-signing our peace pact. We do not anticipate any problems, although we have noticed their ships monitoring the skies in a formation and frequency much different than before. This may be nothing at all, but General Sylus has advised us to raise our level of alert. As you know we are aligned with Pluton and Urellian is aligned with Necruse. We want to create a new alliance and peace pact that encompasses all four planets. As well, we would like you to attend this upcoming meeting, so you can get a sense of how Orgon is governed and learn something about our allies. What do you think?"

"Well I was just going to mention the thing with the Urellian ships before you brought it up. And yeah, I'd love to go to the meeting."

Orb was not known to ramble. "Fine," he said. "Have a good night. I will be in touch."

The screen faded to black.

Chapter Thirty-One

Beal sat at the head of a large ornate table in a conference room on planet Necruse. The room was black and dimly lit. Tamara, Cassandra and the respective heads of Necruse and Urellian were also at the table. Standing behind these seated dignitaries were Urellian guards, some Beal guards and a few Necrusian guards.

Beal had tried unsuccessfully to recruit Michelle and Stephen into his life of lasciviousness. He knew the white circles were offering them a measure of protection, and he knew the Orgonions were behind it. He was disappointed he could not convert Nathan, but pleased he was making a lot of headway with Dave Healy, in spite of the circle.

Healy could not resist Tamara's sexual advances. After a few heated encounters, Beal was pleased to see the white circle on Healy's palm fading, much quicker than the four-month time frame.

Beal knew it was only a matter of time before the circle faded entirely, and then he would have Healy at his mercy. And he had planned on using him as one of his leading warriors in his plan to destroy planet Orgon.

He also planned on converting Michelle and Stephen.

Beal had been going over the plan to destroy Orgon in great detail and had already answered many questions. He had formed an alliance with planet Necruse, offering them unlimited Orgonion resources if they would help him. Necruse leader Monith, a gray reptilian creature resembling an alligator, was receptive to the plan because he was tired of trading his alien creature resources to the Urellians for plutonium and uranium, which they needed for nuclear power. He was also disappointed at his planet's lack of technological development compared to Orgon. Really he was jealous of Orgon's success, and because he was aligned with Urellian and not Orgon, he had to get these resources from the Urellians. They acted as middlemen and profited immensely.

The way Monith saw it, this alliance was a way for him to cut the ties from Urellian, get his resources directly from Orgon and lead his planet to become much more successful, powerful and independent.

Plutoneous, the leader of Pluton, had been deliberately left out of negotiations as all parties felt Pluton was too tightly aligned with Orgon, whereas the Urellian agreement with Orgon was primarily one for defense purposes.

The attack would begin during the peace pact summit meeting. Beal would be disguised as a Urellian. During the meeting they planned on disabling the Orgonion radar tracking devices and sending in Dave Healy to dismantle the Orgon nuclear bomb that was pointed at Urellian.

The Urellian spy ships had discovered the exact location of this bomb and also learned there weren't any others. The respective leaders would stall negotiations, before finally signing the peace pact and new alliance. Once they received electronic communication from Healy that the nuclear bomb had been disabled, they would drop bombs, targeting specific spaceship fleets, military targets, government offices and command central.

They also planned on killing key military leaders and all government officials, including Orb.

Phase two of the plan was to occupy the country with a dictatorship precision and exploit the inhabitants and its resources.

Necrusian leader Monith had reservations, particularly about access to and distribution of Orgon's resources once its government had been destroyed.

Urellian leader Urijah, a green snake-like creature with a head resembling a cobra, also wanted to be sure his planet would get unfettered access to the resources on Orgon.

Finally, both leaders had agreed.

Urijah spoke first. "Okay, okay, I think this will work. We have a few issues to work out with regard to Orgon's resources and my plan of moving some of my people to help govern the planet, but we can revisit this later. In principal, I agree."

Beal nodded. Cassandra sauntered over and began messaging his neck. She displayed ample cleavage. Beal's posture relaxed. He felt very pleased with himself.

It was Monith's turn. "I agree in principal. Although I have an issue with Urellians occupying the planet with too many of their people after we have control over Orgon."

He looked at Urijah, who was emitting a slow and barely audible hissing sound. "What's to prevent you from taking control of Orgon's resources, and extracting my civilian resources in exchange for uranium and plutonium?"

Their relationship was tenuous at best and Urijah knew Monith had always resented his planet for its technological advances, weaponry, and the agreement it had formed with Orgon that essentially allowed the Urellians to exploit the Necrusians.

Urijah's snake-like tongue darted in and out and the hissing grew louder.

Beal interjected. "Come, come gentlemen." He used the term loosely. "Surely you put the proverbial cart before the horse here. I will mediate this thing when it's over and make sure each planet has equal representation and is allowed to extract resources from Orgon. We have a lot of work ahead of us and need to focus on the details of phase one; disable Orgon's nuclear bomb and knock out its government, communications, and key military targets. Everyone will get their share of Orgon's resources, I promise you."

Beal was tiring of this discussion, but Cassandra's talented hands kept him from losing his temper. Tamara had also inched her seat closer to Beal and had begun reassuringly rubbing his leg; occasionally her hand would inch closer to his groin.

Neither Monith nor Urijah had any deep trust for Beal, but they both were more than a little afraid of him.

Urijah wondered if Beal's influence had started him on this path of destruction in the first place but the thought escaped his mind as quickly as it had entered.

Monith wondered the same thing, but also wanted badly to be rid of Urijah's exploitive influence on him and his people. They both nodded and the meeting came to an end.

Chapter Thirty-Two

"Fuck you, you son of a bitch," Dave Healy said, and he heard a bone-cracking sound as he drove his fist hard into the man's nose. The man winced in pain and blood squirted from his broken nose, trickling down his face, and onto Healy's clenched fist.

He was holding the man against a Blue Ford Explorer and his 1968 Triumph TR6 was parked diagonally in front of the man's vehicle, blocking a lane of rush hour traffic on Hastings Street. Drivers slowed as they passed, gawking.

It happened while Healy was on his was to Beal's house for a sex session with Tamara. He had cut the Explorer off, changing lanes without shoulder checking or even looking in his rear-view or side mirrors. The disgruntled man had flipped him the bird and Healy exploded with anger. He had pulled alongside the Explorer, telling the man, in no uncertain terms to "Fuck right off," and "Do you think you own the whole fucking road?"

The man, about thirty pounds heavier than Healy and muscular, responded with a few expletives of his own before speeding away. Healy cut the Explorer off again, this time screeching to a stop in front of the vehicle, forcing it to a stop within inches from his sports car.

He had leaped out of his car, ran to the Explorer and started punching the man through his open side window. He then hauled him out of the vehicle, pinning him to the side of the car where he continued pummeling him now.

"Do you think you own the whole fucking road," Healy asked again between punches. By this time the man's features were barely visible through the mass of blood and cuts. Blood had spattered down his white t-shirt, all over the Explorer and Healy's hands. Healy's arms and shirt were speckled red.

About fifty onlookers had stopped to watch the action and rush hour traffic had all but come to a complete standstill. Nobody intervened but a few people shouted, "Leave him alone."

"Cops," someone yelled. Healy stopped punching the man, noticing for the first time all the blood. He was barely conscious now and stood only because Healy held him up.

Healy released his grip and the man withered down the vehicle, landing on his back on the concrete, his legs bent in an awkward position. "Fuck," Healy said, noticing his golf shirt, shoes, and blue jeans were covered in blood.

One burly bystander finally had enough and approached Healy quickly. Healy noticed the man was about a hundred pounds his better and also held a baseball bat cocked, like Babe Ruth about to hit one out of the park.

Before Healy could react, the bat came swinging toward him quickly. He ducked just in time and the side window of the Explorer shattered as the bat connected with it.

The bat man was distracted momentarily as the victim, now squirming on the ground, was attempting to stand, moaning some barely legible words about his Explorer.

Sirens wailed, the sound growing louder. Healy quickly bee-lined it for his Triumph, hopped in and started it. Bat man pursued him, swinging his weapon as he neared. Healy quickly backed up, the bat swing narrowly missing his windshield as he did. He peeled out, almost clipping his attacker as he found an opening in traffic.

"Holy fuck," he said to himself as he swerved the car into an alley, heading for a side road, where he could make much better time. "What the fuck has gotten into me?"

During the last two months, he had noticed that the effects of the white circle were not what he had hoped, or maybe it was his attitude. He wasn't sure, but he knew he felt good, positive and all that crap, for about two weeks and then Beal had met with him a few times, introduced him again to the many sexual talents of Tamara, and he noticed the white circle had begun to fade rather quickly.

And he noticed his attitude was a lot more aggressive. He often felt anger and rage bubbling just beneath the surface, ready to explode. He examined his hand and noticed the circle was gone.

And he didn't know if he gave a shit as he navigated the vehicle toward Beal's mansion. He cranked up ACDC's *Hell's Bells* and slowly the memory of the incident vanished, his mind returning to the sexual treats that awaited him. He thought of what sexual positions he might try this evening. He knew Tamara was pretty kinky and he doubted she would mind his bloody appearance.

Hell, she'd probably like it.

And, since Healy was the star pupil in Beal's plan to destroy and occupy Orgon, Tamara had been instructed to cool it on the murder attempts. Tamara's task now was to keep him on track, healthy and sexually satisfied, never mind the happy part.

Chapter Thirty-Three

It was June and the weather was sunny and warm. Healy parked his car and walked along the side entrance to the pool. Tamara was stretched out on a lawn chair nude, sunning her desirable body, her eyes closed, a cocktail in hand. She opened her eyes as Healy approached.

"What happened to you?" she said nonchalantly. She sipped her drink as she eyed Healy's blood-soaked body and clothes. He bent down and kissed her, running his hand slowly across her nipples and leaving behind a smear of blood.

She returned the kiss passionately. "Hey, you're ruining my tan," she said matter-of-factly.

"Uh ... had a little road rage incident," Healy said, ignoring the comment. "I'm going to shower. I'll be back."

"Get me another drink," she said, as he slid the patio doors open to the house and disappeared.

He returned fifteen minutes later, hauled Tamara into the grotto and had his way with her for about an hour.

As they returned to the pool with new drinks, Beal and a partially clad Cassandra returned. The four of them sat poolside enjoying cocktails.

Cassandra stripped off her clothes and dove into the pool.

Tamara removed her bikini top and continued tanning, her attractive assets flushed red.

Beal noticed that Healy now had the edge to him he wanted to see. He no longer had a conscience and his temperament had become more and more volatile, thanks to the successful tutelage of Beal, Cassandra, and Tamara.

He told Healy in a few days a Urellian ship would come for them and they would begin a twenty-four hour voyage to Orgon. On board the Urellian ship, there would be a wardrobe change. Healy would dress as an Orgonion patrol agent and Beal would disguise himself as a Urellian.

Healy looked at a picture of an Orgonion patrol agent and a Urellian snake. *Shouldn't be hard for him. He's already a snake.* He cackled loudly at his observation. Healy would occasionally laugh at his own jokes and others would not be made privy to what he was laughing at. Half the time, he didn't know himself.

There was a momentary pause while Beal eyed him strangely. *Not a concern right now,* he thought, *as long as he's not having reservations.*

"So, tell me Healy, are you okay with all of this." Beal searched his eyes for a sign. Beal was as much a master at detecting deception as he was a master of deception.

"Much more than okay. I'm looking forward to it," he said with conviction.

Beal rubbed his hands together, satisfied. Humans are so weak. Such easy targets.

Chapter Thirty-Four

The old woman looked up at Michelle as she read a passage from Ernest Hemingway's *The Sun Also Rises*. She wore a puzzled expression and the cracks in her face deepened as her eyes narrowed.

Not for the first time, Michelle wondered at her choice of novels. Maybe she should have picked something more upbeat, instead of an analysis of the disillusionment and dissatisfaction of a generation of people who grew up during World War One.

After all, ninety-six-year-old Celia grew up during that era and probably didn't need to be reminded of vanishing dreams and goals. But Michelle loved Hemingway's simple but powerful writing style and Celia had agreed to her choice of novels.

Michelle stopped reading. "Is everything okay?" she asked Celia, whose well-worn features had darkened considerably.

"Please continue," Celia said. "I felt some pain in my hip and it reminded me of something that happened to me back then." Michelle decided she wouldn't ask. She did not want Celia's countenance to worsen.

She was on the fourth floor of the extended care unit at The University of British Columbia Hospital.

Since Nathan's departure, Michelle's life had changed for the better, thanks in part to the white circle. She had started volunteering at the hospital, reading, playing cards, talking, and generally entertaining the elderly. She had begun to examine her life and realized how self-centered it had been. It had left her with a hollow and empty feeling and she decided it was not how she wanted to be remembered. *When everything is said and done*, she thought, *a person would not be remembered for their business successes and the quantity of their material possessions. No, they would be remembered for how many people they loved and the depth of that love.*

But she wasn't so sure about Stephen.

He was less self-absorbed and much less sarcastic than before but it seemed to her something was boiling underneath this cool exterior. At times his features would grow dark and Michelle wondered what was going on inside his head.

So far, she had resisted Beal's attempts to convert her. Stephen said he had also rejected Beal's offers. *Do I believe him?*

She noticed Celia had drifted off to sleep, and now the corners of her wrinkled mouth were tilted upwards in a satisfied smile. Lucy the cat had jumped on the bed and curled up alongside Celia's head, purring comfortably. Michelle stopped reading and smiled at the pair. Her mind drifted back to Nathan and she wondered what it would be like to live on planet Orgon.

Chapter Thirty-Five

Nathan fixed his gaze on the large missile and watched as the two guards monitored the blinking computer screens. He squeezed Ophelia's hand tighter and dreaded to think of the devastation such a bomb could produce.

He had just completed a crash course in weapons handling and a tour of the Orgon administration buildings, led by the diminutive Orb. After touring the government meeting rooms, Orb had led them underground via elevator and then through a series of winding corridors and command centers that could be used if the main-floor government offices were destroyed.

Nathan hung on every word Orb said.

He wanted to learn every inch of the government buildings in case he needed that information later. Orb explained the codes used to activate and deactivate the nuclear bomb. He also imprinted Nathan's retina and hand print into the system so Nathan could access the bomb's housing unit to deactivate or activate the bomb.

Nathan had been given complete security clearance for the entire system of government buildings including the backup command centers. It would appear Orb not only had a planned mission for Nathan on Earth, but he also wanted his services on Orgon, if needed. Through a complex system of radar screens, the guards patrolled the skies around the clock and watched for anything that might be considered a threat.

Nathan's curiosity finally got the better of him. "I'm not sure why you're telling me all this."

Orb looked at him long and contemplative and said, "In case something happens to us, we want you to know how our planet functions, at least to some degree, so you can help us carry on. With your contacts on Earth, the information you've learned, you never know when it might come in useful."

"Okay," Nathan said. "Let's hope you can continue your harmonious existence though."

Ophelia looked at Nathan with a worried expression that was missed on the leader of Orgon.

After a brief explanation of the instrumentation used in monitoring the air space, they continued down the winding corridors, up the elevators, and outside into the sunshine. Orb departed, reminding Nathan to be at the meeting at six o'clock sharp.

Chapter Thirty-Six

"What I'm proposing here is not only a peace pact but an accord between all the planets," Orb told the delegation of planetary dignitaries.

They had filed in a few minutes earlier with their respective body guards and were all assembled at the long table in the Orgon administration building conference room.

Orb couldn't shake a feeling of unease as he continued. "Instead of the haphazard alliance we now have, where some planets are excluded in favor of other planets, the new alliance outlines a four-planet union. Which means Necruse will no longer have to go through Urellian to have access to the resources on Orgon. It seems to me Necruse, because of limited access to our resources, has been stunted in its technological development compared to the other planets. As a result, they have lost some of their best minds and are stagnating. The notion of trading ones civilian population for mineral resources is an absurd one, and this alliance will put an end to it."

Necrusian leader Monith nodded his head. If Orb was offering an alliance under which Necruse would be allowed direct access to Orgon mineral resources, what was he doing trying to topple the Orgon government? He twisted in his seat, wondering how he had let Beal and the others talk him into this.

Dressed in Orgonion white, Nathan listened and tried to make sense of it. He noticed Monith's discomfort and couldn't help wondering if something was wrong. He looked at all the dignitaries and studied the bodyguards as Orb talked. His gaze reached the snake-like Urellian entourage and he studied them. Urijah, the leader, had a curious expression on his face and Nathan dried to determine what it might mean. He eyed the bodyguards, noticed one of them regarding him cautiously, and stared at the snake-like creature. The eyes looked familiar. *Where have I seen those eyes before?*

Orb continued. "Not only does this document create equality among the different planets, giving them all a level playing field in which to develop, but it is a permanent doctrine, one that doesn't have to be renewed every four years. It will enable our planets to live harmoniously together for years to come."

Chapter Thirty-Seven

Healy, disguised as an Orgonion patrol agent, examined the series of winding hallways that led to the bomb. To get into the facility, he had already blown the brains out of two Orgonion guards patrolling one of the obscure side entrances. He had cut the eye out of one and placed it up to the retinal scanner, which opened the secured entrance door.

He had blasted the two guards with a silenced nine-millimeter handgun and smiled as their green brain matter splattered. Beal had offered him some fancy laser device but he preferred killing the old fashioned way. He had bought the weapon on the black market a few days before his departure. He had always wondered what it would be like to fire such a piece. And now he knew.

It felt good.

As his next victim walked down the hall, he ducked in a closet and waited. In the dark, he surveyed his piece, making sure the silencer was securely fastened. *These fuckers don't even carry weapons. How stupid is that?*

As the advancing footsteps came closer, he sprang out and leveled the piece at his target's head. The green eyes of the little white creature widened, but only for an instant. Healy took three quick strides, aiming directly between the eyes of his victim, and pulled the trigger with a grin. Green brains splattered everywhere, some of the goo landing on Healy's clothes.

He wiped some brain matter off his arm, pulled out a hand-held computer, confirmed the location of the bomb and continued down the corridor. He estimated five, maybe six more winding hallways and he would reach it. *Guess I could have let him pass, but what the hell. Just one more Orgonion freak that we don't need anyway.*

Chapter Thirty-Eight

Ophelia couldn't shake a deepening feeling of unease as she stared out her bay window and into the sky. The sun was setting and some dark clouds were rolling in. A few Orgonion vessels were in the sky, but the Urellian ship presence had increased tenfold.

She didn't like the looks of it.

Since the tour yesterday with Nathan and her father, she couldn't help feeling something was wrong. She had mentioned it to Nathan after they had arrived home and he shared the same sentiment. He told her he would be extra vigilant at the meeting and would watch for any unusual signs.

But, seeing all the Urellian ships had frightened her to the point of wanting to call Nathan. Or her father.

No, they wouldn't want to be disturbed during such an important meeting. So, she had returned to her computer screen, trying to distract herself by learning more about Earth's history. She wanted to continue to impress Nathan with her knowledge so she made a point of remembering useless trivia. After taking a high-tech virtual tour of some pristine beaches in the Dominican Republic, she had become restless again and was peering out the window.

Finally, unable to contain the feeling of impending doom, she had hopped on her air glider and blasted off toward the administration buildings.

I'll just have a look around, make sure everything is okay. Leaving the last air highway turn-off, she put the vehicle in quiet mode and zipped around to the front of the buildings.

She continued around the convoluted maze of buildings. She glided past ships from Pluton, Necruse and Urellian and noticed some of the ships in the sky had dropped in elevation.

Are they watching me? And why?

She rounded one of the buildings, halfway through completing the perimeter surveillance, and saw them. Two dead Orgonions slumped on the ground, their brains blown out.

She screamed, in her panic accelerating the glider rapidly. She fought to control her emotions and slowed the vehicle down. A small glider appeared behind her and a blast rang out, whistling past her head.

It was a Urellian patroller, firing a high-tech version of a grenade launcher.

He's trying to kill me.

She slammed her glider into high gear, but not before sounding her computerized warning signal. The signal would go directly to Orb and Nathan, who both carried receiving devices.

Chapter Thirty-Nine

Orb bent his head down to interpret the warning that started silently vibrating on his waist. The exact second he bent down, Beal stood up and fired two bullets directly at his head. If he hadn't looked down at the computerized warning signal at exactly that moment, his head would have been blown clean off.

Suddenly gunfire erupted and the room exploded with the cries of battle.

Nathan jumped up and ran for Beal, diving across the table and connecting, tackling Beal onto some guards.

Orb rolled under the table to avoid the barrage of bullets.

Nathan wrestled with Beal, trying to wrest the gun from his hands. Beal held on tightly and the two rolled on the floor fighting for control of the weapon. Finally, Nathan jerked the gun loose.

"You little shit," Beal said. Nathan pointed the gun at his head and then remembered Orb. He glanced behind.

Urijah advanced on Orb, firing as he came closer. In a moment of clarity, Monith pulled out a large sword and sliced off the leader's snake-like head. It hissed as it flew through the air, smacking the wall with a splat, leaving a bluish-green stain.

"We will not revolt. Contain them," Monith ordered his troops, and they started fighting with the Urellian and Beal guards.

Nathan scrambled under the table and grabbed Orb. "Let's get out of here. The bomb. They're going for the bomb."

Orb was frozen in panic. So Nathan tucked the piece in his pants, picked him up and fled, carrying the little leader. Bullets whizzed by their heads as they left, narrowly missing them.

Nathan ran down the hall to the elevator, knowing they could seal off their exit, get to underground central command and the bomb. As they rounded a corner, Orb pressed a button on his waist and a steel door slammed shut behind them, blocking their trailing attackers.

In the elevator, he put the little man down. They could hear bullets ricocheting off walls, screams of carnage, battle and death behind. "Orb, we need guns and we need to get to the bomb control room. Now!"

"Of course," Orb said, composing himself. He entered his secure password and the elevator began its rapid downward descent. "Thank you for saving me."

"No problem. You let all those people in here armed?"

"The Urellians. We have an agreement with them. They're our protectors."

"Not anymore. Urijah just tried to kill you. Please tell me you have a backup plan. And tell me the guards around the bomb are at least armed. And tell me you have a cache of weapons somewhere to arm your troops."

"Yes, yes, and yes," Orb said, opening a metal box fastened to the inside of the elevator by pressing a series of buttons on a computer device attached to his waist. Once opened, he pressed some more buttons.

"I've just opened an arsenal of weapons. Our troops, spaceships and the bomb unit have been notified. As we speak, troops are filing into the lower level and arming themselves for war. Our spaceships are already armed."

"Ophelia says someone broke into the bomb housing sector. How do we know they haven`t disabled the bomb? And where is she anyway?"

"Okay Nathan, now you're the one who needs to calm down. Call her."

Nathan speed-dialed Ophelia as the elevator reached the bottom. No response. He sent a quick message through the device, asking her if she was safe.

Nothing.

They got out of the elevator. The halls were empty. "Where are all the Orgonion troops?"

"Don't worry, they're in the south wing," Orb said.

Orb quickly opened another hall panel, extracting a large machine gun. He handed one to Nathan, along with a handgun.

"I'm going further underground to command central, this way," he said, handing Nathan a tracking device. "This will lead you to the bomb housing unit. It's the other way. Go, make sure it hasn't been disarmed or compromised. I tried the guards, but the communication panel is down. You'll also know where I am at all times with that tracker."

They went their separate ways. Nathan flung the machine gun over his shoulder, sprinting toward the bomb housing unit. He was thankful that during his tour of the administration building, he had also been given a crash course on how to use the weapon. He didn't know how much time he had and worried about Ophelia.

Chapter Forty

Healy heard all the commotion and picked up his pace. He had stealthily approached the last guard before the door to the bomb, pointed the weapon at the back of his head and blown his brains out.

The guard had been pressing some buttons on a panel when the bullet had abruptly ended his life. The shot penetrated straight through his egg-shaped head and blasted the control panel, knocking out communication to the wing. Healy pulled out his hunting knife, cut out the man's retina and placed it on the scanner beside the last door. It whirred open. The two guards stared at their intruder wide-eyed. They were unaccustomed to battle. And, they were afraid to fire for fear a ricocheting bullet would blow them straight to Pluton.

Healy didn't have the same fear. He fired two bullets into each guard's head. One guard got off a shot before dropping and it singed past Healy's head. They withered to the floor, leaving a trail of brain matter plastered to the wall behind them.

Healy smiled. *I'm getting good at this.*

Nathan heard shots ring out as he neared the door. He had already passed three dead bodies in the corridor so he knew what he was up against; someone who would not hesitate to kill. He rounded a corner and saw Healy studying a hand-held computer, at the same time fidgeting with computerized controls lining the wall.

He pointed his machine gun. "No you don't, Dave."

Healy quickly leveled his piece at Nathan without dropping the small computer.

He paused. There was a flicker of recognition of old times, an old friendship. But Nathan could see in the eyes this was no longer his friend.

Beal had taken over his psyche, turned him into a madman.

But maybe some hope. The flicker of recognition. He could at least try.

"Dave, put down the weapon, put your hands up."

There was perhaps two seconds of hesitation before Dave grinned. "What, you think we're old buddies still? That I'm just going to listen to you? I like this life."

"You like killing people? That what you signed up for?"

"I'm going to be rich beyond all imagination. Have all the most beautiful babes I want, whenever I want. You should have taken it while you had the chance."

"It's not what you want, Dave, to kill people. You never signed up for that. Come off it. You made a mistake, you killed some aliens, but this isn't Earth. Did you know they reform criminals on Pluton. Maybe you can go there, get reformed."

Healy only grinned. The flicker of recognition had disappeared. He was much too far gone to ever come back.

Before firing, he winced slightly, a tell.

Nathan dove at the same time two bullets whistled past his head and sprayed his friend with a hail of machine gun fire. Healy jerked spasmodically as the bullets penetrated, finally crashing into the panel of computers behind him, and wilted to the floor.

Nathan kneeled over his friend, propped his head up. Healy's mouth frothed blood and he gasped for breath. He was trying to say something. Nathan sat him up, the blood drained from his mouth. His eyes were sad and they were the eyes of his friend.

In a last dying gasp, he said, "I'm sorry."

Then his eyes glazed over and he went limp. Nathan slowly rested his head on the floor, brushed a tear from his eye and turned his attention to the computer screen.

Chapter Forty-One

The red digital numbers on the computer monitor read fifty-nine seconds until detonation.

Until detonation! What! Healy must have accidentally hit the detonation sequence instead of the deactivation sequence. Nathan dropped his weapon, scrambled to his feet and dashed over to the emergency control panel in the corner of the room.

The main panel had been too badly damaged by the hail of bullets and sparks flew out and popped.

He remembered the system had a backup panel in case of power failure. He reached it, imprinted his hand. The panel door did not open.

Thirty-six seconds and counting.

His heart raced. What was wrong? He straightened his hand out, wiped the sweat off on his pants, slowly returned it to the metal imprint reader. The door opened.

Twenty-nine seconds.

The code. *What was the sequence of numbers?* Orb had just told him yesterday and now he couldn't remember. The oval roof activated and opened. The protective glass case around the bomb lifted automatically.

How far would it launch before detonating? Nathan didn't know. He tried an eight-digit combination.

Nothing.

Thirteen seconds.

The oval roof continued to open. The bomb whirred into motion and slowly began ascending.

Think. He had attached letters to every number so he would not forget but now he couldn't remember the letters.

This was a system he had used on university exams. For a third-year university sociology exam, he had attached a word to every concept the professor had said would be on the exam. He had formed the words into a ridiculous sentence which he memorized. When he sat down to write the exam, he wrote out the entire sentence, then each concept that each word represented and went to work finishing the exam. The result was an A+, the highest mark in the class. So he knew the system worked. It just wasn't working now.

Five seconds.

Then the letters came to him. ABRCUVIG. And the corresponding numbers. 32654217.

Three seconds.

He frantically punched in the number combination, hoping his memory hadn't failed him.

One second.

He heard a soft, monotone female voice. "This explosive device has been deactivated. To reactivate for readiness to Urellian, please proceed with emergency backup activation sequence."

He sighed. He had prevented it from blowing up but now it was deactivated. He heard a large bomb blast and the shell shock blew him against the wall, debris raining down on him.

He slowly got up, wiped blood from a cut on his forehead and rushed back to the panel. *Shit, they know it's been deactivated, and they're dropping bombs.* Another bomb blast echoed a little farther away and the building shook violently with the force.

Nathan steadied himself, remembered the activation sequence and punched it in.

The same voice: "This explosive device is now in a state of readiness, destination Urellian. Thank you and have a nice day."

The oval roof closed, the bomb lowered and the glass protective case re-emerged, encasing it.

Chapter Forty-Two

Nathan ran to the exit. The corridors shook. *If bombs are still being dropped, someone must not realize there is a very big bomb pointed at their planet? Or maybe they don't care?*

His tracker beeped and he stopped. Orb's face came into view. "Good work Nathan, I received a signal the bomb has been reactivated to Urellian."

"Well someone doesn't realize it because they're bombing us."

"They bombed the communication tower, so I can't broadcast it to them. For some reason, their tracking systems aren't alerting them to it."

"Or they don't care."

"Listen, one of the buildings has a backup communication system, but the power is down. There is another power supply that can only be turned on manually. It's the eighteenth unit in E-wing. Punch it in your tracker to locate it," Orb said.

Orb sounded unusually calm but Nathan knew he was more than three thousand feet underground, defending with the help of a large computerized control panel and very far away from immediate danger. *That's okay. That's where he should be.*

"What about Ophelia?" Nathan asked.

"She doesn't have a tracker with her so I don't know where she is."

"She sent us a signal didn't she?"

"It must be broken. I'm not reading anything."

"Well I'm sorry but before I do anything, I'm going to find her."

"Okay, I'll try and get another team on the communication system. Good luck," Orb said.

Orb's image went black as Nathan reached the elevator to the main exit. He stepped in and ascended six floors and exited. As soon as the doors opened, he was met with gunfire by Urellian forces.

He scrambled to the ground, firing his machine gun. Two bodies dropped dead, and he got up, scrambling toward the main exit doors. He checked for his handgun and found it still nestled in the crotch of his pants.

Outside was carnage. A couple of the administration buildings had been severely damaged by the bomb blasts. Fires raged. Debris and bodies were strewn all over the ground. Some limped along bleeding, others screamed for help.

Plutonians, Urellians and Necrusians also made up the dead and injured. A black air glider zoomed in and hovered directly in front of Nathan, leveling a gun at his head. He quickly blasted off a few rounds. The Urellian driver died instantly, slumping over in the seat. The air glider to the ground and came to a smooth stop. The driver fell out in a heap.

Nathan darted for it, climbed on and zoomed away, in search of Ophelia, the communication wing, and Beal, in that order.

As he soared overhead he got a better glimpse of the destruction. A bomb had destroyed the north corner of the government offices, and part of the south wing had sustained some blast damage.

Smoke swirled, fires flared, warriors battled.

A few ships had been shot out of the sky, the wreckages now coming into view. Machine gun fire echoed through the sky as pockets of resistance on the ground battled for territory.

More armed Orgonions, now in green military fatigues, were exiting the government buildings. The Urellian resistance grew smaller. They were outnumbered two to one by the Orgonions and Necrusians.

The Plutonians had fled or were fleeing.

Nathan scoured the area in search of Ophelia. He heard a whistling sound behind him, glanced back, steering the craft hard right as he did, and narrowly escaped being blown up by a large missile. He accelerated immediately as his attacker came in hot pursuit.

He weaved in and out, up and down, as the air glider tailed him, firing missiles and bullets.

A few months into his stay on Orgon, he didn't know the Venice settlement real well. As the air glider inched closer to his ass, he wondered why he hadn't decided to take a few sojourns into the countryside with Ophelia, get to know the terrain a bit better.

The university route. That's it. He veered a sharp left as an exploding missile decimated a building beside him, narrowly missing his air glider. He knew the Orgon University route by heart and he doubted he could say the same for his pursuer. He cranked up his elevation, gave it full throttle. The pinging of bullets slicing through metal. His air glider had been hit. He swung the glider around, shooting.

A few bullets sliced through the flying machine behind him and he felt better. But only a little. This bastard was going to kill him. And he wasn't going away easily. Terrain whizzed by him as he dug into the recesses of his mind for a plan.

That's it, he thought. *A three-sixty.* He had seen Weelie do it once in an acrobatic show with his air glider but Nathan wasn't sure he could repeat the performance. He pointed the nose straight up and hit the turbo. The glider shot up ninety degrees, the enemy hot on his tail.

Don't know how fast this machine can go but I guess we're going to find out. He pulled hard on the steering controls trying to make the glider come out of the ninety, go into a curve. It was still going straight up. He pulled harder. Finally, the machine started to arc in a circle. The Urellian snarled, firing off more rounds. A few bullets sliced into Nathan's machine, inches from his leg.

But the enemy was losing steam now as he dropped behind. He either had no stones or his machine couldn't take the abuse.

The motor started whining as Nathan completed the 360-degree turn. The planet grew bigger much too fast. He wasn't going to make it. He rocketed downward toward Orgon, jerked frantically at the controls, leaned back in the machine, trying to sway his momentum. His pursuer was nowhere in sight. He descended rapidly. The motor stuttered briefly, then caught and twenty or so feet before crash landing, the glider righted itself.

"Whew." Nathan wiped the sweat from his brow. "A little too close for comfort."

He could see his pursuer in front of him now, trying to locate him. It was too late. Nathan raced up behind the Urellian in an instant and discharged several bullets in the back of his head. He slumped over, bluish-green goo oozing from the fresh head wound, and the glider crashed to the ground, exploding into a huge fireball.

He heard a beeping sound, glanced down at the tracker fastened to his waist, and saw Orb.

"Nathan, I know where she is."

He put the glider in cruise control. "Where?"

"She's trapped somewhere in the university. I just got off the line. She has at least two Urellians after her."

"I'm on it," Nathan said, grabbing the controls and accelerating toward the university. It was just over the next plateau, a few minutes away.

He brought the glider to a smooth landing on the university lawn, jumped off and ran toward the front entrance. Just before he reached it, he saw a missile speeding toward his head. *Not another one!*

He dove into the open front door, and the bomb exploded into the side of the building. The shell shock and force blew him twenty feet inside the hallway, where he finally skidded to a stop, dust and debris crashing on top of him. He shook it off and stood up groggily.

Sharp pain. His right leg. Something was wrong with it.

He saw the blood first, soaking his pant leg, then the metal piece, the size and diameter of a fire poker, protruding out. The blast had shot the chunk of metal right through his calf. He bent down and examined the wound. Fortunately, it hadn't penetrated the bone.

He listened for approaching footsteps.

Nothing.

He stumbled into an empty classroom and with every step felt excruciating pain. Blood squirted from the wound. *I'll lose too much blood if I leave this thing in here.*

He sat down, set his machine gun down and ripped the sleeve from his shirt in two pieces, rolling up one piece in a ball and inserting it in his mouth. The other piece he put on the floor. He took a deep breath, bit down on the ball of cloth, and yanked the metal debris out of his calf muscle in one swift movement. Blood spewed forth like a gushing faucet and he winced in pain. He grabbed the other piece of cloth and cinched it around his leg as a tourniquet.

He finally exhaled, seeing the blood flow had slowed noticeably, if not stopped altogether.

Chapter Forty-Three

He stood, strapped on his machine gun, adjusted his handgun and slowly crept down the hall. Rocket fire, gun blasts, and screams echoed from outside. It had turned into a full-scale war. He rounded a corner and heard a sound. Footsteps. Someone was coming. Two Urellians emerged from around the corner, firing shots. Nathan ducked, pulled out his handgun and fired two shots, hitting one in the chest and the other in the head.

They both dropped to the floor, the Urellian who had been hit in the chest still shooting bullets as he landed. He leveled his firearm at Nathan, who sidestepped the bullets and shot the enemy twice in the head.

He heard a scream, faint but decipherable. *Ophelia?* The sound came from the floor above him and Nathan scrambled up the stairwell in pursuit. He scanned the corridors, listening.

Then he saw two Urellians at the far end of the hall outside a closed door.

A spray of bullets penetrated the door from inside the room and they jumped back, pausing before returning fire.

A scream, this time louder and more panicked. *Definitely Ophelia, trapped inside the room. It's only a matter of time before they burst through the door and kill her.*

"Over here, you fuckers," Nathan said, pointing his handgun at them and firing two shots. Both bullets missed and the snake-like Urellians regarded him angrily. Hissing, they charged down the hall.

Nathan ducked into a classroom and waited in the corner, lying down in sniper position, his machine gun pointing at the open door. *Come in, come in, you son of a bitch.*

The footsteps neared. One enemy popped his head in the door, spraying bullets and retreated. Nathan didn't have time to get off a shot. The bullets shattered the windowpanes above him and shards of glass rained down.

He rolled in time to avoid being severed by some of the bigger pieces, positioned himself under some desks. A Urellian leaped in the doorway, a rattle of bullets announcing his untimely arrival.

Nathan pointed his machine gun at the legs, spraying gunfire as he did. He chopped the legs out from under him and the Urellian landed with a thunk, still blasting off rounds.

Nathan rolled, shooting as he went. The Urellian hissed loudly and went limp, after a trail of bullets penetrated his body and head. The other enemy appeared as his comrade went limp, jumped up on the desks and started firing down at Nathan, who began twisting and rolling underneath, trying to avoid the gunfire.

A shot rang out. He hissed, toppled over and impaled himself on the protruding shards of glass in the damaged window. Blood squirted out of his mouth and the room grew silent.

What? Where did the shot come from?

He stumbled to his feet and saw Ophelia leaning against the doorway, smoking gun in hand. She had shot him in the back of the head. Her large green eyes were wide, her little hands trembling with fear. Nathan limped over and the couple embraced.

"Are you okay?" he asked.

She stared into his eyes, tears welling. "I'm scared."

"You saved my life."

"What happened? Your leg."

By this time, Nathan's pant leg was saturated in blood from the knee down. "I'll be okay, don't worry."

Unable to contain her emotions, Ophelia started crying, the tears running freely down her face.

Nathan wiped her face and kissed her. "It's okay. It'll be over soon." And he had no idea if his words even vaguely resembled the truth. "Let's get out of here."

Chapter Forty-Four

Sitting in a command chair in a Urellian spaceship, Beal barked out orders to the crew. Cyclops, military commander and replacement Urellian leader, had let Beal run the show to this point but he was beginning to have his doubts.

"There, over there," Beal pointed toward the communication tower.

When the battle broke out, he had exited the government offices with Cassandra and Tamara and boarded the Urellian ship. They had focused bombing efforts on destroying the government administration buildings, but incoming Necrusian and Orgonion ships had forced them well outside the perimeter of the government offices.

So they indiscriminately bombed residential settlements until Cyclops had presented a map verifying the location of the backup communication tower.

Beal had received a signal the bomb had been deactivated from Urellian, but then communication with Dave Healy went dead. He had received another signal the bomb was reactivated, but he had surreptitiously disabled the Urellian control panel. He didn't care if planet Urellian was blown to pieces. He wanted Orgon destroyed and Nathan dead.

The spaceship hovered above the communication tower.

"Ready the bomb," Beal said to Cyclops, who signaled one of his crew and the target was locked in.

Chapter Forty-Five

Orb and ten of his most trusted advisors worked busily underground, monitoring computer screens, dispensing attack orders, watching the efforts of the team sent in to restore communication to the backup tower. So far, the first battalion sent in had been annihilated by Urellian air support and ground troops.

He sensed they knew the bomb had been reactivated and was again pointing at Urellian; but either they didn't care, or somehow Beal was sabotaging their signal.

In any event, at this juncture he was unwilling to destroy planet Urellian until he was satisfied they had been given fair warning.

"Orb, can you hear me?" It was Necrusian leader Monith.

He noticed the transmission came from the backup tower. "Monith, did you restore communication?"

"Yes, my troops entered from the back, while yours were getting slaughtered in front."

Orb paused, the realization sinking in of how ill-prepared he had been. "Thank you," he said, waving to General Sylus to send out full warning signals immediately. He clicked the line dead as the warning signal transmitted.

Chapter Forty-Six

"What's taking you? Drop the goddamned bomb," Beal urged Cyclops. The commander raised his hand to give the order, furrowing his leathery brow.

A voice cut through the Urellian monitoring systems. It was also audible outside the spaceship.

"This is Orb. We have reactivated our nuclear bomb and it will destroy Urellian if you do not cease fire immediately. I repeat, cease fire immediately or Urellian will be destroyed."

The addlepated commander hesitated.

"Drop the bomb, he's bluffing," Beal said.

A crew member walked to a monitor to verify the threat, noticed it had been tampered with and motioned to Cyclops to wait. He waited while the Urellian flicked switches, adjusted controls and the screen came to life.

It beeped loud and clear, signaling imminent danger. The soldier motioned to Cyclops, who put his hand down, glaring at Beal.

Beal backed into a corner of the ship, Tamara and Cassandra assembling behind him.

"This must be some mistake. I thought there was no bomb threat to your planet."

Cyclops immediately gave the order to the entire fleet—ground and air warriors—to cease fire.

The order was transmitted to Orb, who in turn told his troops to stand down.

Cyclops ordered his troops to retreat, board their ships with the dead and wounded and leave Orgon immediately.

Beal pressed a transmitter on his hip pocket and a black spaceship zoomed into view, circling the Urellian vessel.

Cyclops, his eyes narrowing and green knuckles balling into fists, pulled his handgun from its holster, leveling it at Beal. He fired and Beal grabbed Tamara, pulling her in front of him as a shield.

She shrieked and dropped to the floor as the bullet pierced through her neck, narrowly missing Beal. Tamara grabbed her bleeding throat, gasped and spewed blood, uttering a guttural "aaaaaaaaaaaaaaaaahhh" as she died.

The loudspeaker from the black ship reverberated. "Do not take any further violent action or your ship and crew will be destroyed."

Cyclops, about to fire again, paused.

"I wouldn't do anything, unless you all want to end up like her," Beal said, pointing to the lifeless Tamara.

Cassandra stood jaw-dropped staring at the corpse of her friend. She glared at Beal. "What's wrong with you anyway?"

"It was her or me, honey. Now shut up unless you want the same fate."

Cassandra's eyes narrowed.

The loudspeaker on Beal's ship blared. "Open the door immediately or we will disable your ship and kill you."

Cyclops gave the order and the large steel door opened. The black ship inched closer, dropping a platform.

"Now, we're going to get on that ship and you aren't going to do a damn thing," Beal said.

"As you wish, but your day will come," Cyclops said. "And I hope I'm around when it does. Ready the defense system, arm the missiles."

Beal and Cassandra inched toward the platform, the atmosphere tense and quiet as all eyes watched. As they reached it, Beal shoved Cassandra aside, stepped in front of her and boarded first.

Cassandra tripped on her stiletto heels and Cyclops fired a shot intended for Beal. But he was already inside the ship, the door closing. The bullet hit the metal frame of the ship with a zing and flew into space.

Beal glared at Cyclops, flipping his index finger.

"Wait for me," Cassandra said, kicking off her high heels and running. The door was closing as she made the platform, and there was only a small opening remaining. She dove for it, a little too late. Her torso was severed in half, blood and guts squirting out as it twisted spasmodically in the vice-like grip of the automated door.

A muffled scream echoed from inside Beal's ship as the bottom half of her torso jerked loose, bounced off the ascending platform and flew into space.

The engine thundered into high gear, a fireball of exhaust blasted the Urellian ship, and Beal disappeared.

Chapter Forty-Seven

Pursued by two Urellian gliders, Nathan flew around the Orgon University, Ophelia clinging tightly to his back, when he heard the announcement. He veered the machine hard left to avoid a large missile and watched as the missile blew up an Orgonion dwelling, the gut-wrenching screams of its airborne residents punctuating the ashy sky.

But for the crackling of flames, pain-filled screams, and the hum of engines, a semblance of quietude prevailed. No more bombs and bullets. His attackers had vanished.

He righted his course, steering the craft toward the administration buildings, noticing Urellians exiting as he approached.

"I think it's over," he said to Ophelia, the discomfort of her tight grip starting to cramp his chest. She sensed his discomfort, loosened her vice-like attachment. "Where are you going?"

"To the government buildings."

She hugged him tightly again. He winced and she loosened her grip.

Orb stood outside with an entourage of armed guards as they approached. Monith and a few of his soldiers lingered at his side. Nathan couldn't see a single Plutonian and by this time most of the Urellians had fled.

Soldiers and medical personnel were busy attending to the dead and wounded and fire crews doused flaming buildings. Nathan brought the craft to a smooth landing and Ophelia jumped off and ran into her father's arms.

Nathan acknowledged Orb with a wave but didn't waste any time with idle talk. A large section of the government building was on fire and a crew was on site spraying the smoldering flames with a white foamy liquid.

They dragged the injured and dead from the building. Zipped-up black body bags lined the perimeter of the fire. Nathan, his leg injury still smarting, limped over to help.

"Where are you going?" Ophelia asked.

"They need help."

"We need to get you to the medical wing," she said. Monith and Orb watched Nathan curiously. Both of them held electronic devices, and in between surveying the damage they barked out orders to their respective subordinates.

"I'll catch up with you later," Nathan said. "People are dying."

He approached a beefy Orgonion in a silver metallic suit who stood and ordered the crew around.

"What can I do?" Nathan asked. The chief eyed him curiously, pointing to his blood-soaked leg and rolling his eyes. "You can get yourself to a hospital."

"Later. You look short of men. Where do you want me, sir?"

"It's Chief," the man said.

"I can see that."

"No, my name is Chief."

"Oh. I'm Nathan." He extended his hand and Chief offered his. "Go over to that truck and grab one of these suits. Then, at the back there, there might be more people. Have a look. If you want."

Nathan walked over to an aerodynamically designed silver fire-fighting vehicle, opened a side hatch and removed a fireproof suit. As he put it on, Ophelia waved to him while accompanying Orb and Monith back into the undamaged side of the building.

Nathan felt the searing heat as he neared, stepping over rubble and bodies as he entered the flaming inferno. Beads of sweat instantly formed on his forehead and he was soaked in seconds. The acrid odor of burning flesh assaulted his nostrils.

The suit offered some protection, but Nathan suspected if he got too close, it would burn or he would pass out from the intense heat. He paused, took a couple of deep breaths, struggled to control a nauseous feeling and continued.

"Over here," a silver-suited firefighter yelled. "They're trapped." One of the corner offices was completely engulfed in flames. Horrific screams echoed from within.

The firefighter had his hose trained on the office and the white foam sputtered out. But, it was no match for the advancing flames. As Nathan got closer he could see the firefighter's protective suit was stained charcoal-grey from the fire.

"Listen, I'll put the hose on that part there, where it's not as bad, maybe you can go in? People are dying in there, can't you hear?"

Nathan nodded his head, listening to the screams, which by now had become shrieks of panic. "Okay hit the area, and I'll go in."

The man turned the hose to a small black hole, a tiny area the flames had yet to claim.

Nathan took a couple deep breaths and ran for it, white foam trailing him and flying overhead. He crashed through the burning office and focused. It was black with smoke and red with fire. He couldn't see anything and he felt the heat burning his eyes and suit.

Chunks of debris fell around him as he crunched his way toward the screams. *If I can't see, let the sound lead me.* Then a sudden gust of wind blew in, fanned the flames and cleared away some smoke. He saw a couple crouched in the corner, hugging each other. They were on fire, burning from the bottom up. Their terrifying screams pierced his heart.

He glanced behind him at the spraying firefighter. "Closer, come closer," he said. "They're on fire. Here, quick, bring your hose over here."

The firefighter advanced and a ball of flame swirled and blasted him. He backed up to avoid being engulfed, tripped. The hose wiggled on the ground like a snake, hissing forth its foam in squiggly lines.

Nathan walked toward the screaming couple. The woman looked at him, raw fear and pain in her eyes, and waved. The man did the same. Nathan was horrified at the image in front of him but plodded forward, the heat so intense he thought he would melt.

What are they waving at? And at once he saw it. The man reached down and pulled out a crying Orgonion baby. They were protecting their infant.

In an instant, Nathan took three more steps, grabbed the infant, turned and ran from the building. The fallen firefighter had retrieved his hose and guided Nathan out in a shower of white. He handed the crying baby to another firefighter who had approached with a fresh hose and spun around to return.

But it was too late.

He saw the entire office completely engulfed in flames. The ceiling came crashing down, raining debris everywhere. The haunting screams continued, eventually faded and disappeared as the trapped victims met a fiery death.

"Are there any more in there?" Nathan asked the firefighter, who was now on his knees with exhaustion, still spraying foam.

"I don't think so."

Another truck screeched to a halt, six suited men jumped out and began fighting the blaze. Overcome with exhaustion, Nathan dropped to his knees and stared silently.

Finally, the men began winning the battle and he left.

All he could think about as he walked into the government building was the whereabouts of Beal.

What was his next plan?

Chapter Forty-Eight

"Give me some more," Alisa Stevens said, brushing her flowing brunette hair away from her eyes. She knelt down staring at the three lines of coke remaining on a mirror on the scarred coffee table. She was coming down and didn't want to have to think about the grim reality of her life right now.

"Hold your horses, chick," Mark Dredsky said, inhaling a thin line of the white powder through the plastic funnel of a disposable Bic pen. "There's only two more left."

"I know. I want one."

"Okay, here," he said sliding the mirror over to her. Twenty-six-year-old Alisa grabbed the Bic and snorted the line quickly up her nose, rubbing it afterward with her index finger and thumb. She wiped the thin white film onto her tongue and sat back staring out the small window at the rain pelting down outside.

It was early evening and she was in a run-down, one-room apartment on East Hastings or skid road, a seedy area of Vancouver populated by the homeless, drug-addicts, hookers, an assortment of other derelicts and criminals.

The daughter of a wealthy family living in the British properties, her life had been going well until she met Beal, who lived two doors down from her. He had introduced her to drugs and wanted her as part of his entourage. She had initially resisted but eventually his seductive charms were too much for her and she had begun making love to him regularly and doing coke often. Shortly after, she broke up with her six-year boyfriend and got fired from her position as an oil executive.

She was an attractive woman with an easy smile, sharp brown eyes, clear complexion, soft facial features, and an athletic and attractive body. Except now, after a couple weeks of drug abuse, she had lost a little weight and developed large black circles under her eyes.

Aware that Beal was leading her down a dangerous path, a few days ago she had left her parents' house. Looking for drugs on skid road, she had met Mark, a drifter and petty criminal who had provided her with a fix and a roof over her head. It didn't take long before she ran out of money and started providing sexual favors to Mark in exchange for coke.

In his forties, he was a motley character with long straggly hair, a pockmarked complexion, and a quick temper. It was the quick temper that got him fired from his warehouse job. He had punched the foreman in the face after being accused of being stoned on the job. His father was an abusive alcoholic, his mother a schizophrenic pill popper.

He had lived on the streets or in shitty apartments since he was fifteen.

Sometimes he would leave the dingy apartment and return four or five hours later with a wad of cash. His business—fencing hot goods for an Asian gang.

"I'm going to the bathroom," he said, getting up and wiping some debris and papers off the faded and torn brown couch. "Don't fucking do that last line."

"Why do I even bother with this strung out bitch," he muttered to himself as he opened the door. *Oh, right she has a smoking hot body and she gives good head*. He smiled, exposing rotten teeth as he closed the door behind him.

Chapter Forty-Nine

Beal walked up the creaky stairs of the ramshackle rooming house. It didn't take him long to find her. He had a sixth sense about these things. He had spent a couple of hours walking the streets, instinctively knowing she would come here in need of a fix. He had threatened a few people and quickly learned her location.

He knew she was with some other idiot but he didn't think the loser would present much of a problem.

He wasn't in a good mood by the time he arrived at room 404. He kicked the door. It flew clear off its hinges and landed on the floor with a loud clapping bang. He stepped over it and entered.

Alisa's jaw dropped as she saw him. She was about to say something and he put his finger to his lips.

"What the fuck," he heard Mark say from the bathroom.

Beal ran to the bathroom door and stood just to the side. He unsheathed a military-style combat knife and raised it in the air, ready to attack.

Alisa screamed.

"What the fuck is going on he ..." Mark said, as he opened the door and stepped out. But he didn't get to finish the sentence. Beal brought the knife expertly across his throat, slicing his jugular vein with a clean precision movement of his hand.

Alisa screamed again, stood up and ran for the door.

Mark grabbed at his throat as the blood squirted out. He stumbled back, crashing into the wall, slithering onto the floor.

He tried to speak. But, as he died all that came out was a gurgling sound as blood squirted from his mouth and filled his lungs.

Beal sheathed the knife, raced across the room and grabbed Alisa by the arm. "Don't scream or you die," he said, choking her with his free hand. "You stick with me, everything will be fine. You don't, well, not so fine."

She shivered in his grip.

"Are you going to relax?" he asked. By this time he had his other hand over her mouth.

Wide-eyed, she nodded.

"If I take my hand away, you won't scream now will you?"

She nodded again and he released his hand from her mouth.

"Good," he said, and kissed her full on the lips. She winced.

They exited the building, climbed in a waiting black limo and headed to Beal's mansion.

Chapter Fifty

A few hours later, Alisa was freshly showered, wearing a transparent negligee and lounging on a couch in Beal's mansion. She was comfortably numb, but in the recesses of her mind she was plotting an escape. She didn't like Mark much anyway but felt traumatized at his death.

About ten lines of coke later, it was fast becoming a distant memory.

Beal stoked a raging fire after they had made love, finished, and poured a glass of Glenlivet single malt Scotch—neat.

"Would you like one, honey?" he asked Alisa.

She smiled, trying not to make it look forced. She knew if she demonstrated disinterest or dislike it would mean trouble.

"Sure, sweetie," she said. "On the rocks."

He walked over and handed her a drink, they clinked glasses and kissed. Beal sat down in an armchair and admired his latest acquisition.

The death of Tamara and Cassandra meant he had to recruit at least two more lovers—he had an insatiable appetite for sex. He had his eye on another one but had yet to close the deal—it was Nathan's friend Michelle. He had been stalking her and had noticed there was some discord developing in her relationship with Stephen. He was convinced Stephen would be an easy mark and wouldn't mind sharing.

Michelle on the other hand would be a challenge.

Since his arrival a few days ago from Orgon, he had been busy plotting his next moves. He was infuriated that Nathan had stymied his plot to destroy Orgon. In the process, his fragile alliance with planets Necruse and Urellian and had also been ruined. It didn't help that he disabled the Urellian monitors, recklessly dropping bombs on helpless Orgonions.

What cratered his alliance with Urellian was largely his own doing. He had failed to tell Commander Cyclops that Healy had ultimately failed in his attempt to dismantle the bomb and it had been in a state of readiness pointed at Urellian. But it wasn't his fault that Necrusian leader Monith had a change of heart at the last minute and had beheaded former Urellian leader Urijah.

He knew Monith had an axe to grind with the former leader so it didn't surprise him. What did surprise and infuriate him however was that Monith had also taken sides with the Orgonions and out of the blue taken up arms in their defense.

What also infuriated him were Nathan's heroic actions—which had effectively kyboshed the entire operation.

The deaths of Cassandra, Tamara, and Healy were simply collateral damage and he didn't give it a second thought.

Next move, next move. He prodded his mind forward, sipping the Scotch and admiring Alisa's beauty. She seemed to read his mind and smiled.

Convert Michelle, Stephen, corrupt Earth with a vengeance and go after Nathan and planet Orgon. Possibly convert Earthlings to take up round two of the Orgonion battle. Not necessarily in that order.

The seeds of a plan were beginning to grow and he grinned, satisfied that he would find a viable solution.

Chapter Fifty-One

"I have to go," Nathan said. "They're my friends. What do you think he's going to do with them?"

Ophelia looked blank. "I don't want you to leave me."

It was their first argument. They sat in the kitchen of their dwelling occasionally looking out the window as they talked. Luckily their house had been spared any serious damage during the war, but a bomb had exploded on the front lawn, leaving a large crater where there was once a well-maintained garden. It served as a permanent reminder of the carnage that now existed on planet Orgon; and a bitter symbol that their utopia had more than a few chinks in the armor.

Since the battle a few weeks back, Nathan had been busy helping to rebuild Orgon. His leg was healing well and, while he still limped a little, doctors had told him he would be fine in a month. It was still wrapped in a bandage.

All his classes had been suspended while the university was being rebuilt and he no longer worked at the mine. The rebuilding effort was top priority. According to his verbal contract with Orb, tomorrow was his last day on the planet. It would be three months to the day. And, while his relationship with Ophelia was progressing, he had started to worry about his friends, Michelle and Stephen.

When Orb had told him Beal had escaped, he knew Beal would be plotting his revenge. Who knew what his next move might be? But Nathan felt certain it would mean more deaths.

Their discussion had revolved around Nathan's plans to return, but Ophelia didn't want him to leave. It had started friendly enough. But, as she became more and more adamant, it had gotten quite heated.

Nathan was getting frustrated with her inability to understand. He took a few breaths, trying to calm himself. Ophelia had her back to him now and just stared out the window.

Then a light bulb came on. *What do you expect her to say?* Even though Nathan wasn't sure he was capable of being with someone as sweet as Ophelia long term, or even live on planet Orgon long term, he thought he loved her.

He tried again. "Listen, honey, I'm sorry about all this." *If all else fails, say you're sorry.* "I promise that after I'm done on Earth I will be back."

She spun around and smiled. "For good?"

He had told himself previously he wouldn't lie to her. And so far he had lived up to his words. "I can't say that right now, but I will be back. I promise. Let's just see how things go."

It was an answer Ophelia wasn't satisfied with and she frowned, turning and gazing out the window again.

There was a knock at the door. They both turned. "Are we expecting anyone?" Nathan asked.

Ophelia turned, frowning. "No."

Nathan automatically glanced at the security camera. But then he remembered, the system was still down, the result of the explosion. He went to a window and peered out. The burly firefighter he had encountered earlier stood at the door, a bundle wrapped in his hands.

Nathan opened the door. "Chief," he said.

"That's right. It's Nathan, right?"

Nathan nodded and looked down at the package. It was a small baby girl. Her little green eyes opened and she smiled at Nathan.

By this time, Ophelia stood behind him, smiling at the little girl.

"This is the baby you rescued from the building," Chief said. "As you know, her parents died in that fire and there is no other family to look after her. Do you want her?"

Nathan gave Chief a puzzled look. "I ... I don't know."

But Ophelia had already stepped forward, took the baby from Chief, and now she caressed her head lovingly while the child giggled.

"What's her name?" Ophelia asked.

"Chloe," Chief said.

"What a beautiful name," she said, carrying Chloe into the house. "Come in."

"I can't, I have too much work to do. You don't have to decide right now, but please would you mind looking after her for a while? Orgon is still in shambles and we need time to find suitable parents if you don't want her."

Ophelia looked at Nathan for a response. "Just for a while, honey, until we decide?"

What was he supposed to say? He was leaving tomorrow for Earth anyway and he wasn't even sure how long he would be gone. Besides, although he wasn't a fan of kids, he enjoyed how Chloe brightened Ophelia's mood.

Besides, Chloe was cute. "Okay, sure, why not," he said.

Chief smiled. "We'll talk more in a few weeks," he said, waving as he turned around and left.

Chapter Fifty-Two

Nathan helped with debris cleanup for a few hours before heading over to see Orb. He climbed off his large backhoe which he was using to shovel debris into dump trucks. A few days after the war ended he had made some inquiries about his friend Weelie and discovered his home had been blown up by a bomb, killing him and his family.

The body count was approximately 10,000 Orgonions, 3,000 Necrusians and 11,000 Urellians. With the sophisticated technology these planets had, it didn't take long to rack up the dead.

About 6,000 were among the injured, and about 2,000 of those were Urellians that had been shipped off to secure hospital facilities on Pluton. Orb was in the planning stages, but had yet to negotiate with the Urellians to facilitate the release of these prisoners.

He had yet to decide his next move.

Orb sat in the underground control center amidst a buzz of activity doing exactly that when Nathan entered. Dressed in metal battle armor, Sylus was at his side and the two studied computer monitors while other technicians worked feverishly at individual computer screens. Orb stopped working when he saw Nathan. He extended his hand. "How's our hero doing?"

"I'm fine," Nathan said, although he didn't feel like a hero.

Sylus, a hulking man of about three hundred pounds, extended his hand. "You keep that up we're going to find a permanent home for you here."

Nathan smiled. "Can we talk somewhere more private?" he asked Orb.

"Sure," Orb said, pointing to a new dot on the radar screen and asking Sylus to determine its origin and identity.

He motioned Nathan into an office, closed the door, and they sat down.

"How are we doing with everything?" Nathan asked, getting right to the point.

"By that you mean?"

"I mean do we know if the Urellians are going to plan another attack for one?"

"I don't think they'll try that now that we have the bomb pointed at them. It would spell their complete destruction."

"Does your intelligence indicate they may form another alliance with Beal?"

"No, we've been watching his activity and he hasn't approached the Urellians. Besides, the new leader, Cyclops, wants him dead for betraying the Urellians."

"What about Pluton? Are we still tight with them?"

"Absolutely. When war broke out they fled for their lives, and that's all they did. They weren't in on this conspiracy, if that's what you're wondering. Besides, they depend on the alliance with us for protection. They have no nuclear capability, no army."

"And Monith and the Necrusians?"

"Monith was in on the conspiracy, but he changed his mind because he liked the sound of the new alliance. He liked it because it gave the Necrusians direct access to our uranium resources. And, Monith never liked Urijah much. The two didn't see eye to eye."

"Which leads me to my next question," Nathan said. "How tight are we with the Necrusians?"

Orb paused before answering. "Well, I can tell you this much; we now have a bomb trained on them. We've learned their military and nuclear capability is much greater than we gave them credit for."

"Okay, since Urellian once guarded your skies in exchange for resources, whose doing it now?"

"We are," Orb said. "We've implemented a new radar technology, I was just going through some of the points with Sylus, and we have a number of patrol ships airborne. As well, since the war we've begun manufacturing another fleet of patrol vessels."

"That's a good idea," Nathan said. "I don't think you want to be unprepared like before. What about Beal and the very real threat he still poses?"

"I thought you would eventually lead to Beal," Orb said. "I also realize your three months are up and we've barely had time to teach you Orgonion customs."

"Oh no," Nathan said. "I've learned a lot. A couple things. Do you still want me to stay here, learn your ways, and teach them to humans on Earth?"

"In light of current events, that idea needs further consideration."

"Okay, let me ask you this: I have to go back to Earth, deal with Beal. Do you even want me back on your planet?"

"Yes," Orb said. "Ophelia has grown quite fond of you. You're welcome back any time."

Things were becoming clearer to Nathan. "Let's get back to Beal. Can you tell me what he's been up to?"

"It looks like he's corrupting and converting everyone he possibly can."

"And my friends, Michelle and Stephen?"

"So far they're safe."

"Yeah, so far," Nathan said. "Does he have plans for Orgon?"

"I imagine he does. People like him don't go away."

"No, they need to be killed. And that's one of the pressing things on my mind. Do you think I can sleep at night knowing my friends and my planet are in grave danger? That I can just go on my merry way learning about everything here when my planet is ready to go to shit?"

"I imagine it would be difficult."

"Well help me Orb. Help me kill Beal."

The little man became somber. "I told you the only way Orgonions can go to war is if we're defending ourselves."

"Well don't you think this qualifies?"

"He isn't attacking us."

"He's planning on it."

"That's not the same."

Nathan thought maybe a diplomatic tactic would work. He knew he would have a formidable battle on his hands with Beal and he also knew Orb had a highly sophisticated and well-trained army. He wanted to bring in a little swat team of his own to bring him down, knowing he wouldn't stand a chance on his own.

"What exactly are you proposing?" Orb asked.

"I was thinking maybe you could volunteer a handful of your best men, a spaceship or two, and we could travel to Earth and take Beal out. I can't do it on my own. And, you said you want to save Earth anyway, so isn't that what you'd be doing?"

There was a long pause. "Okay, Nathan, I owe you for saving our planet. Two spaceships and twelve of our best men. When do you want to leave?"

"Soon."

Chapter Fifty-Three

Michelle was leaving her volunteer job at the senior citizen facility when she saw the eyes watching her.

It was dark and rainy.

The man stood across the street, an umbrella in hand. She couldn't make out his features clearly. *Who the hell is that?* Her car was parked about a block away. She turned and walked briskly toward it. She walked about ten steps, turned around.

He followed her.

Panicking, she ran across the street and a vehicle screeched its tires and honked as she froze like a deer in the approaching headlights. She dropped her purse. She bent down to pick it up and Beal was upon her.

"Let me get that for you," he said, bending down and picking it up. Some of the contents had spilled out onto the wet pavement and he collected them.

"Beal," she said. "You scared me."

"I'm sorry," he said seductively.

The driver rolled down the window of his beat-up pick-up truck. An unshaven and grizzled head stuck out, an unkempt mop of curly brown hair framing it. "Why don't you watch where you're going?"

Beal handed Michelle her purse with contents. Grabbing for it, her right hand with the circle slid over Beal's hand. He winced. *Good. It still works.*

"Why don't you shut the fuck up," he said to the driver as they walked to the curb.

Maybe it was the authority in the voice or the malicious glare that accompanied the remark, Michelle didn't know, but the man rolled up the window and sped away without saying a word.

"Thanks, Beal," Michelle said. "Listen, what do you want?"

"Oh, I'm having a party at my house on the weekend and I thought you and Stephen might like to attend."

"I'm sorry but we're busy."

Beal's seductive and diplomatic countenance changed. "Oh not to worry, it's going to be going on real late, so you can come over when you finish what you're doing."

Michelle wasn't one to mince words. And she was tired of this forced politeness. "No, Beal, we can't come and we don't want to come. Do you think I'm stupid or something? I heard what happened to Healy at your party. And, by the way, where is he now?"

"He met a rather unfortunate end I'm afraid."

"He what?"

"He's dead, Michelle, and unless you and Stephen want to end up the same way I suggest you reconsider my offer."

Michelle fingered her keys from inside her purse. She wanted to get out of here fast. She opened the driver's door, slid into her blue 1998 Toyota Corolla.

Beal's limo pulled up, stopped in the middle of the road. "If it's any consolation, Healy died a hero for the cause," he said, before she closed her door and sped away.

The rain hissed down as she drove. The wipers were on full, but they were no match for the pelting rain. Her hands shaking at the wheel, she pulled over, put the car in park and took a few deep breaths.

She slowly loosened her white-knuckle grip on the wheel, released her right hand and fumbled in her purse for her cell phone. Finding it, she dialed her boyfriend. It went to voicemail, and she left a message for Stephen to call ASAP. Michelle hated the acronym and only used it in an emergency. She tried the pub's land line where Stephen bartended.

A waitress picked up the phone. Her voice could barely be heard through the background hum of conversation and laughter. "King's Castle Pub, Annie here." Michelle remembered Annie as the new blue-eyed blonde. She might have a curvaceous figure, perfect teeth and attractive features, but she wasn't the sharpest tool in the shed.

"Annie, it's Michelle. Can I speak to Stephen please?"

The line went static. "I'm sorry I can't hear you."

Louder. "Can I talk to Stephen please?"

More background noise. Finally, "Uh, he's really busy right now, can you call back later?"

"Can you tell him Michelle called, tell him to call me as soon as possible?"

"Sure, no problem," Annie said, hanging up.

Michelle doubted Annie would remember to forward the message, pulled into traffic and steered her car downtown toward the pub. Just as she turned onto the Lions Gate Bridge, the car sputtered and stalled. She tried starting it. Nothing. She turned it over a few times to no avail. Finally, she looked at the gas gauge. Empty.

"Shit," she cursed, realizing she had forgotten to fill the tank when she had left home that morning. Her mind had been too preoccupied with Stephen's increasingly dark mood swings.

Chapter Fifty-Four

"Why don't you come over for a drink?" Beal asked Stephen. The little pub was packed and Beal had to raise his voice to be heard.

A bubbly brunette sat next to him. Her eyes were glazed and she slurred her words when she spoke. She was half in the bag.

"One second," Stephen said, mixing another drink.

Annie came behind the bar and smiled. "Someone called for you, I think."

"Who was it?"

"Uh," she looked at her tray of drinks as if the answer was somewhere there. "Sorry, I can't remember."

"Any message?" Stephen asked, placing a drink on the counter for a patron. "Five-fifty please." The man threw down seven dollars. "Keep the change."

Annie studied her tray. "I can't remember. I don't think so."

"Don't sweat it, sweetie," he said, winking at her.

He returned to Beal. It was the third time Beal had visited the bar. And Stephen was warming to him. The angle he used was money. Beal promised Stephen a salary and position which would make his current income look like chicken shit. He had tried to get him over to discuss it and so far Stephen had refused. But he felt the man weakening and knew it was only a matter of time before he had him under his spell.

"Sorry, Beal," Stephen said. "Too much noise."

Beal was whispering something in the drunken brunette's ear. She giggled as he looked at Stephen.

"Well, you wouldn't have to put up with all this noise if you worked for me, now would you?"

"I don't know. We've never actually talked about what I'd be doing."

"We can discuss that at my place tonight." He handed Stephen a card. "You remember where it is?"

"Oh yeah," Stephen said, remembering the hotties he had encountered on his last visit. "Excuse me," he said, acknowledging a customer's order. He pulled out a bottle of beer, popped the cap, and placed it on the bar, imagining a lascivious sex scene in Beal's grotto.

For some reason he hadn't found Michelle all that sexy lately although she was attractive enough. She had brown eyes, thick, flowing reddish-brown hair, a mischievous grin and a quirky sense of humor. And she was eager to please in the bedroom.

"Five-fifty," he said, taking the twenty dollar bill and making change. Putting down the change, he said "Thanks."

But Michelle was the farthest thing from his mind as he returned to Beal. "Sure, why not," he said. "Mike will be here in a half hour. I can leave then."

Beal polished his Scotch. The drunken brunette had one arm around his shoulder and the other hand roamed around his leg. She kissed him on the cheek and giggled.

"Isn't he handsome?" she asked Stephen.

Stephen suspected the hand had already found a few other places to roam. He nodded.

"See you when you get there," Beal said, throwing some money on the counter and helping the brunette out of her seat and out of the pub.

"What's your name, honey," he asked the bombed brunette as they stood on the sidewalk waiting for the limo.

"I'm Tammie," the woman said. "You?"

"Beal," he said. "And I'm charmed." He kissed her hand as the limo pulled curbside. "Let's go have some fun Tammie," he said, hoping she was exciting as the late Tamara was in bed.

Chapter Fifty-Five

"Watch this," Beal said to Stephen as they sat in his limo curbside on busy Robson Street at three in the afternoon the next day. Beal stepped out of the car, grabbed a pedestrian by the arm, squeezed and stared into his eyes. The well-dressed businessman's expression changed instantly from calm and pleasant to unpleasant.

And crazed.

With glazed eyes, he approached an old woman, snatched her purse and ran down the street waving it and screaming wildly.

"Wow," Stephen said from inside the car. "It's that easy?"

"After you get good at it, yes. You can see it in their eyes if they'll bend."

They walked on.

"Here's another one, wait." Beal approached an attractive mid-forties woman, smartly dressed in a beige business suit. "Hello, ma'am," he said, offering his hand.

The large-breasted woman stared curiously at first, then extended her hand and smiled. She had red hair done up in a bun and it framed her pleasant face nicely. Her deep green eyes had a twinkle in them and she looked intelligent.

They shook hands and Beal stared. Her pleasant smile turned into a mischievous grin. She dropped her purse, tore off her suit jacket, stripped off her white button shirt and undid her bra, exposing a perfect pair of large breasts.

She smiled at Beal. "Do you like?"

"Very much," he said, fondling them. Pedestrians had stopped to gawk and before long there was a large male contingent ogling the exhibitionist display. After some whistles and loud clapping, she picked up her purse and proudly marched down the street, leaving her clothes behind.

Stephen stood outside the car, grinning. "Very good. When are you going to teach me?"

"In time, young man, in time. Here, let's try something else."

He walked up to an attractive mid-twenties couple walking down the street laughing, holding hands. He shook both of their hands, and they stopped, their eyes glazing over. They walked to a large garbage can, tipped it over and rolled it into the glass storefront window of a high-end clothing boutique. The window shattered as the steel container rolled right through it. The two laughed wickedly, joined hands and skipped down the street, singing something indecipherable.

A diminutive Asian man appeared, cursing in Cantonese. He balled his fists and ran after the pair.

Stephen leaned against the limo chuckling and watching the display as Beal walked into a cigar shop.

It had been two days since Stephen had been at work. After Beal had left, Michelle had called a couple more times and Annie said he had left.

And Stephen had refused to answer her calls to his cell phone. He didn't know what to say to her and he wanted a glimpse of Beal's world. He had spent two nights at the mansion and had partnered up with Tammie. A heavy drinker, she had proved to be everything Stephen had suspected in bed.

He had initially hoped that after two days he would return to Michelle, beg forgiveness and resume his life with her. But the temptations Beal had offered proved to be too much—frankly he was enjoying this new life. He never bothered to call his boss at the pub and Beal had already advanced him two thousand dollars.

Michelle had rung Stephen's phone constantly but had yet to show up at the mansion. He was sure she knew where he was. He was going to throw the cell phone in the pool but Beal assured him very soon Michelle would be invited over.

Somewhere in the recesses of his rational mind he thought her arrival would not be pretty.

Chapter Fifty-Six

The moon was full as the two white spaceships entered Earth's atmosphere.

Nathan sat in the control room of one of the vessels and reviewed the plan with Sylus. In the two days that Orb had assigned Sylus to his care, the two had become friends. Nathan admired the general for his courage, loyalty, and strategizing skills.

Nathan had been given a quick course on Orgonion warfare, had been put on a special strength-enhancing protein diet, and been given another crash course on weapons handling.

Sylus wore his signature silver metal battle gear and the rest of the team wore green military fatigues and black army boots. They all had special steel helmets with built-in night vision goggles and communication devices attached. Nathan had a machine gun slung over his shoulder, a large knife, grenades and two handguns.

He hoped he didn't have to use them.

According to Orb, these twelve represented the very best warriors Orgon had to offer.

Approaching Earth's atmosphere, Nathan had used a tracker to call Michelle. She was fit to be tied. "Don't worry," he had told her after being briefed on the situation. "We have a plan."

He had instructed her to stay calm, call Beal, and say she had reconsidered his offer and would like to discuss how she could help.

The plan was to locate her at Stanley Park, arm her with fog grenades and have her drive to the mansion. Once she entered, she was to pull the pin and when the melee ensued the special forces would storm the building and capture or kill Beal.

Sylus pointed to the rendezvous point on the map. "So this is it then?" he asked, in his booming baritone voice.

"Yes. We come in here. Give Michelle the grenades here, then take off and land here."

Sylus nodded. "We're almost there. How much time?" addressing one of the pilots.

"Five minutes, sir."

Chapter Fifty-Seven

Michelle checked her watch as she steered her car through the winding road that snaked through Stanley Park. *Five to seven. Good. I have time.*

Since Stephen's disappearance, she had called in sick from her secretarial job and had spent two sleepless nights worrying, smoking cigarettes, and drinking coffee. A phone call to the police had netted zero results.

She had been just about to jump in her car and drive to the mansion when Nathan had called. She had bawled her eyes out on the phone. Her nerves were frayed and she was exhausted—physically and mentally.

Noticing her knuckles turning white, her hands stiffening, she relaxed and swerved into the rendezvous point. "Get your shit together, girl."

The trees loomed large, casting grossly exaggerated shadows over the marked parking stalls. The parking lot was empty.

She killed the motor, lit another cigarette, got out, and waited.

The full moon illuminated the ocean waters a dark metallic silver. The gentle waves lapped up the sandy shoreline. Twigs snapped in the nearby forest and she jumped back, screaming. Her cigarette dropped from her hand and rolled along the pavement.

Yellow eyes regarded her curiously. A raccoon.

"You scared the crap out of me, little guy," she said, reaching down to retrieve her smoke.

Suddenly she heard a high-pitched whistling sound. Then she saw them. Two glowing white objects descending, becoming larger.

UFOs? Not. I know who they are. "Identified flying objects," she said, as the vessels swirled and hovered. One landed while the other remained hovering.

Nathan stepped out with a small package. She dropped her cigarette and ran to him. He smiled as he saw her getting nearer, put down the package and embraced her with a bear hug. He saw worry creasing her features, black circles under her bloodshot eyes.

"How are you, Michelle?" he asked, searching her face.

"Uh, well you know, could be better."

"Don't worry, this will all work out."

She lit another cigarette and offered him one. Although he had been off them for a few days as part of his training, the temptation was too much. "Sure," he said, and she lit him up.

"How's Matty?" he asked, picking up the package.

"Great, real good. I love that cat. I think she's the only thing keeping me sane these last few days. Always cuddling and so assertive."

"That's Matty," Nathan said, producing two black devices. "Okay, here's the pin, see?"

"Yeah."

"Now, when you need to activate it, you pull this and throw it. After you pull the pin you have less than a second to release it. Got it?"

"Right."

"The fog is harmless so don't worry about that. But, figure out where you're going to go before you pull it because you won't have much time afterwards. Get under a coffee table or in a closet. Is all this clear, Michelle?"

She was shivering. "Yeah, it's all good. I'll put them in my purse."

"Here's something else." He handed her a little red piece of plastic with a toggle switch. "When you throw the grenades, you flick that little switch there. It will send a signal to us and we'll know to go in."

She examined the little device, put it in her pocket, and nodded.

"Don't worry," Nathan said, hugging her. "Everything will work out."

Chapter Fifty-Eight

The spaceships hovered high above the mansion and the team watched as Michelle entered. Sylus and his men detected several armed guards on the perimeter, on rooftops and circling the mansion on foot. A half a dozen pit bulls also roamed the property.

"Okay," Sylus said, "hit the invisible shield and bring us down right over there, behind the house."

Michelle clutched her purse tightly as the doorman let her in. A short hallway opened into a large living area. She made a mental note of the large closet on her right. Stephen, Beal, Tammie, and Alisa were lounging on the couches beside a raging fire. The two women wore panties, their naked breasts exposed. They all had drinks.

They wore confident grins except for Alisa. She had a devious expression as if she was hatching a plan, waiting for an opportunity.

Stephen jumped up and smiled. "Hi, honey, you're home."

His eyes did not look the same. They were glazed over, distant and cold.

He kissed her on the cheek. "May I take your purse, babe?"

"No, no," she said, clutching it.

"Okay, what you got in there, a bomb or something? How about a drink?"

"Sure, honey."

"Rum and Coke okay?"

"Fine."

He walked to the bar to fix the drink and Beal motioned her over to the couch. "Come and sit down," he said, patting an empty spot next to him.

She decided it's now or never. She pulled the toggle switch out of her pocket. She fished the fog grenade from her purse, pulled the pin and rolled it over to where Beal and the women sat. Flipping the toggle switch, she ran for the closet and closed the door behind her. The room was instantly enveloped in a thick layer of fog. She heard screaming, shouting and swearing. For good measure, she opened the closet door, pulled the pin and tossed the other grenade into the living room.

Chapter Fifty-Nine

"Let's go, men," Sylus said. They removed the invisible shield from the vessels, the doors popped open and they stormed out. Machine gun bursts instantly lit up the night sky.

Sylus was the first out. He liked to get his hands dirty. He gave the order and four of his crack shots took out the guards on the rooftop. They fell to the ground.

Five of the team including Nathan ran to the rear door.

Nathan shot an approaching guard in the head before turning and firing on a pit bull that had clamped onto the back of his pant leg. The animal squealed, fell and went limp. He saw another guard emerging from the door shooting and he shot out his legs. The man fell to his knees but continued firing.

A team member shot two bullets that struck him in the head and he slumped over twitching for a few seconds before dying.

Nathan donned his fog lenses, kicked the corpse off the porch, and entered the house. A guard came around a corner firing randomly. He was an easy mark. Nathan unloaded three bullets into his head and he crashed into the wall and withered to the floor, smearing the wall red.

Along with the team, he moved into the living room, searching for Beal. He could hear machine gun fire outside as the rest of the team battled with Beal's men.

Three of the team members dispersed upstairs, and Nathan searched the living room. Tammie and Alisa were huddled in a corner, white with shock.

"Stay here," Nathan ordered. "You move you might get killed."

"I want no part of this shit," Alisa said. She couldn't see six inches in front of her face.

"Don't worry, we'll get you out of here. Where's Beal and Stephen?"

Tammie didn't say a word.

"I heard footsteps going up the stairs when the fog came," Alisa said.

"How many sets?" Nathan asked, the main floor exploding with gunfire.

One of the team members emerged. "This floor clear, Nathan. Five dead. None of ours."

"I don't know," Alisa said. "There was yelling and screaming. Could have been one set. Could have been two. I can't be sure."

"Okay, okay," he said, heading for the stairs. "Don't move. Stay with them," he added, addressing the remaining team member.

Nathan ran up the stairs almost tripping over a dead Orgonion in his haste. *Shit*. He ran into another one of the team. "Did you find them? Is it all clear?"

"This floor is clear. Seven dead, including one of ours. There's a firefight on the roof. Maybe four of the enemy."

Nathan hurried to the end of the hallway, saw the circular metal stairwell leading to the roof, and began the climb. He scrambled to the flat surface, bullets screaming past him. Sylus was behind a metal outbuilding. Blood squirted from his leg and had formed a little pool on the gravel surface.

"What's going on?" Nathan asked.

"There's four of them on the other end of the roof, behind or inside that brick building. Stephen and Beal include the four. We've taken down four of their men, lost one. My team leader radioed all the outside men and dogs are down."

Bullets pinged into the metal building. Nathan put his machine gun down, ripped his shirtsleeve into shreds and tied a piece onto Sylus's leg to stop the blood flow.

"There, that should do it." Sylus didn't flinch.

"Any orders, boss?"

"Yes. We toss a fog grenade over there, put the glasses on and go in for the kill."

"What about Stephen?"

"Collateral damage. We have to get out of here before the police show up."

"No disrespect, Sylus and I won't disobey a direct order, but will you give me a shot at saving Stephen?"

"What are you proposing? And make it quick."

"I'll try calling Beal out, get him to surrender."

"He'll never do that. Have you forgotten who you're dealing with?"

"Just one chance. If it doesn't work, your plan."

"Okay," Sylus said, rolling into a sniper position.

"Beal," Nathan shouted. The firefight continued. "Beal! It's over, give yourself up." The gunfire stopped. Sylus ordered two team members to stop shooting.

"It's never over, Nathan, haven't you figured that out yet? Are you stupid enough to think it will stop at me?"

"You're over, Beal. We've got you surrounded. All your men are dead. Give yourself up and we'll spare your life." Gun drawn, Nathan stepped out from behind the metal building. He turned to Sylus. "Cover me."

"Fuck you," Beal said. The door to the brick building sprang open and he jumped out clutching Stephen in a chokehold. He had a gun pointed at his head. "Call your men off!"

Stephen's expression was calm. He could have been watching figure skating on TV.

Nathan leveled his gun at Beal's head. Sylus stepped out, gun drawn.

"Call all your men off or he dies. Put that fucking gun down," Beal said.

"Put the gun down, Beal. It's over," Nathan said.

"Do you think you'll get rid of evil if you get rid of me? It's like fucking terrorism, buddy. You kill one and there's five more to replace them. Don't you get it, won't you ever get it. Evil is an inherent part of human nature."

Stephen reached for Beal's gun and Beal pulled the trigger. A shot rang out, barely missing Stephen's head. They struggled toward the edge of the roof, wrestling for control of the weapon. As they got to the edge, Stephen yanked the gun from Beal's hands and shot him in the eye. Brain matter, skull fragments and blood blew out the back of his head.

Beal stumbled backward, grabbed Stephen by the arm and they fell off the roof, plummeting to the concrete driveway below and landing with a thump.

The two guards sprang out of the brick building and Sylus cut them down with machine gun fire. They only got two shots off and the bullets strayed to the sky. They never had a chance.

Nathan heard sirens.

"We have to go, right now," Sylus ordered, slinging his gun over his shoulder. "Pack it up, men, get ready to leave," he said into his tracker.

The troops mobilized and ran back through the house.

Most of the fog had disappeared.

Chapter Sixty

Nathan sat quietly on a bench seat at the back of the ship, patting Matty. The cat meowed and licked his face.

Michelle sat beside him. He put his arm around her. Tears rolled down her face. He kissed her on the cheek.

Alisa sat beside Michelle, occasionally wiping away a tear. She shivered from cocaine withdrawal.

Sylus was in the control room having his leg attended to by a doctor.

The two Orgonion corpses were in a freezer awaiting cremation on Orgon.

After all the killing was over, Michelle and Alisa had decided to come to planet Orgon. Alisa had insisted she needed to get her life in order and wanted a fresh start.

Michelle, devastated at the loss of her soul mate, didn't see a lot of options ahead for her and decided to help with the rebuilding effort. So she had packed up a few belongings and boarded the spaceship. She took some consolation in the knowledge that ultimately Stephen had died a hero.

Nathan knew it wouldn't be a perfect world on Orgon. It was far from the utopia he had envisioned. But it was a planet he could now call home. He knew he had a long way to go, but he was now on the right path.

Earth would always have its problems. Unless a major shift in thinking were to occur, its people would continue to destroy it. Maybe Beal would be replaced by someone more powerful, more evil. Who knew?

But, he wasn't sure he was the one to solve Earth's problems. Only time would tell.

Meanwhile, there was still a massive rebuilding effort that needed to be completed on Orgon. And, with the alliance shattered, a new pact would have to be formed—one much different than before. Who knew how the balance of power would shake out?

One thing Nathan did know. He wanted to return to Orgon.

Matty meowed. She wanted attention. Nathan handed the cat to Michelle.

"Can you hold her for a second, sweetie? I want to check on Sylus."

"Sure," she said, taking Matty. The cat instantly curled up on her lap and purred. Michelle smiled in spite of her pain. Alisa kissed Michelle tenderly on the cheek.

Nathan entered a private control room, approached a computer screen, pressed a series of buttons and the image of Ophelia fluttered to life. She sat on the couch nervously watching the object of her desire.

"Hi honey," Nathan said.

She smiled tentatively. "How did it go?"

"For now everything's taken care of." He wouldn't go into the details until they were face to face.

There was a momentary pause. "Where are you?"

"I'm in the ship with Sylus."

Another long pause.

Finally Nathan said, "Baby, I'm coming home. For good."

Ophelia beamed, a single tear forming on the edge of her right eye. "You mean it?"

"I do. I love you."

"I love you too."

"See you soon," Nathan said, pressing a button and watching the white image of Ophelia fade to black.

He went into the ship's main control room. Sylus sat studying computer screens pensively, oblivious to his leg injury. Doctors had finished attending to him.

"How are you?" he asked as Nathan approached.

"I should be asking you. You're the one with the injury. How is it?"

"It's nothing. I'm a quick healer."

There was a moment's pause before Sylus regarded Nathan somberly. "We've got a long way to go, don't we?"

"Miles to go. But we'll make it. I know we will," Nathan said.

He put his hand on the big general's shoulder. "You know, when I think about it, I guess I was meant to be on Orgon with your people. I think when I started getting into trouble with booze and women it really became a foregone conclusion."

The general looked at him, puzzled. "Did you say Orgon Conclusion?"

Nathan thought about it for a moment. "Yeah ... I guess I did."

Also by William Blackwell

Freaky Franky Preview

"If you're looking for a horror with a slice of religion, I recommend this book. It's one of the greatest horror novels I've ever read and it's not a cliché plot. I rate this book 10/10." Goodreads

When an enigmatic town doctor saves the life of Anisa Worthington's dying son, she abandons Christianity in favor of devotion to the cult of Saint Death. Some believe the mysterious skeleton saint will protect their loved ones; help in matters of the heart; provide abundant happiness, health, wealth and justice.

But others, including the Catholic Church, call it blasphemous, evil and satanic.

Anisa introduces Saint Death to troubled Catholic friend Helen Randon and strange things begin happening. One of Helen's enemies is brutally murdered and residents of Montague, a peaceful little town in Prince Edward Island, begin plotting to rid the Bible belt of apostates.

Anisa suspects Helen is perverting the good tenets of Saint Death but, before she can act, a terrible nightmare propels her to the Dominican Republic in search of Freaky Franky, her long-lost and unstable brother, who mysteriously disappeared without a trace twenty years ago.

To her horror, Anisa learns Freaky Franky is also worshiping Saint Death with evil intentions. As a fanatical and hell-bent lynch mob tightens the noose, mysterious murders begin occurring all around Anisa. Unsure about who's an enemy and who's an ally, she's thrust into a violent battle to save her life as well as the lives of her unpredictable friends and brother.

About the Author

Canadian dark fiction author William Blackwell studied journalism at Mount Royal University and English literature at The University of British Columbia. He worked as a journalist for many years before pursuing his passion for storytelling. His novels have been characterized as graphic, edgy, and at times terrifying. Currently living on a secluded acreage on Prince Edward Island, Blackwell finds much of his inspiration from Mother Nature, odd people, traveling, and bizarre nightmares.

Author Comments

Thank you for reading this book. I would be eternally grateful if you would post a book review on your favorite book retailer website. A positive review is the highest compliment a writer can receive. Reviews are crucial to the success of any author. You don't have to say much. A few sentences will suffice.

In other news, I have a gift for you. Complete the signup form contained in the link below with your name and email address and download a FREE copy of *Resurrection Point*, a dark tale about the horrifying consequences of experimenting with death and resurrection. You're only agreeing to be kept up to date on blog posts, new releases, and freebies. I promise I won't spam you and you can unsubscribe at any time.

Thanks again for your support.

http://www.wblackwell.com/free-ebook/